Christmas at Turtledove Place

SUGARPLUM FALLS BOOK THREE

JENNIFER GRIFFITH

Christmas at Turtledove Place

Sugarplum Falls Romance

Book 2

Jennifer Griffith

Christmas at Turtledove Place

ASIN: B08N5B2TSS
ISBN: 9798562575920

This is a work of fiction. Names, characters, places, and events are creations of the author's imagination or are used fictitiously. Any resemblance to actual persons, living or dead, events, or locations, is purely coincidental.

Cover art by Blue Water Books, 2020.

For my friends Juli and Britlyn

"The earth has grown old with its burden of care, but at Christmas it always is young

The heart of the jewel burns lustrous and fair, and its soul full of music breaks the air

When the song of the angels is sung." –Phillips Brooks

Chapter 1

Sophie

Despite the fact that she'd been forced this morning to turn the calendar to show December first, the worst day of the year, she couldn't deny the palpable excitement in the therapy room of Darlington Speech Clinic. Colored lights of the desktop Christmas tree blinked off and on, matching the thrill of what was about to happen with Lachlan. *He's going to learn it today. I just know it.*

Sophie ignored the dozenth chime of a text from her phone. Instead, she handed Lachlan Llewellyn, age seven, a lollipop. Never had a kid been named something so difficult by unwitting parents. They could have had no idea their child would be unable to pronounce the letter *L.*

"Okay, Lachlan. Take this lollipop and stick it behind your top teeth. Press a little. Do you feel that ridge?"

Lachlan slurped. "I wuv woot beer fwavor."

"Run the lolly back and forth a little. Did you find the bump? It's a little line." She waited until his eyes lit up. "Good! You got it. Now, take the lollipop out for a bit and see if you can still taste the root beer right on that line."

It took a second, but Lachlan nodded quickly. "I got it. It onwy tastes a witt-o wike woot beer, so I got to add mow." He stuck the all-day sucker back in his mouth to re-coat the area. That was fine. This was all supposed to feel like a game to him. "Okay, teach-o. I'm weady."

"Good job, buddy. Now, with your tongue sticking right on the line, breathe and feel the air going down both sides of your tongue. Got it?" He had

1

it. "Now, turn on your voice at the same time as the air going through." It took a few tries, but pretty soon, Lachlan could make the sound, and even added a La-La-La-Lachlan at the end.

"Teach-o! I think I got it!" He made about a hundred *la-la-las*, and even broke into the chorus of "Deck the Halls," which, apparently, they'd been practicing already in his first grade music class. "I can say my fa-la-las now." He threw his arms around Sophie.

"I bet you know what your homework is going to be."

"Singing Chwistmas songs? And saying my whole name?"

Yup. He knew the drill. They'd work on his *R* sounds next time.

"Thanks, Miss Hawkins. I love you."

Sophie loved him, too.

Lachlan's mom collected him, her eyes wide as she heard his demonstration. "Wow, Lachlan! Great job!" Then she turned to Sophie. "It's like an early Christmas present. Thank you."

As soon as she passed her boards and received her certification, she'd be a full-fledged speech therapist, and Dr. Vaughn could offer her a real position at Darlington Speech Clinic, instead of just as his unpaid intern.

And sort of his girlfriend.

Hmmm.

Should I be dating my boss? Probably not. For several reasons.

Another text sounded. Who was blowing up her phone? She pulled it out. All of them were from Vronky. All of them read *Family emergency. Family emergency.* Yikes.

Sophie left the therapy room, but Nurse Jodi sped toward her. "Oh, there you are, Ms. Hawkins. Your roommate Veronica is in the waiting room. She seems distraught."

Uh-oh. Vronky had never come here before. In the deserted waiting room, Vronky rushed to her holding a tube of some kind.

"What's wrong? Is someone sick?"

"Yes. Very sick." She lowered her voice. "And depraved. Can we go somewhere to talk?"

So, not physically sick. What could be going on? Sophie followed

Vronky out into the cold day on the cusp between autumn and winter. No snow yet, but soon. Cars roared past on the busiest street in Darlington.

"Are you all right? Is it your family? What's the emergency?" Her stomach clenched. "Is it *my* family?"

"First off, are you okay? You had to flip the calendar to the D-word."

"I'm okay." Well, she had been, until Vronky brought up the painful truth. Moving a piece of paper once a year should not activate trauma memories. Geez. A full twelve years ago today, but that should be long enough to forget the teen trauma. When would Sophie ever get over her older sister's wedding?

"Good. Because you won't be." Vronky looked almost haggard. "The family emergency is all yours." She slapped a paper cylinder against Sophie's hand, and it unfurled into a magazine. Then she launched into one of her diatribes. "Seriously? Why would Tracey pick Nero of all people? He's the greasiest, most disgusting thing to happen to Southern rock since that guy bit off a bat's head on stage."

Gross, and that stunt probably hadn't happened in Southern rock. Whatever, an aging rocker like Nero had nothing to do with the Hawkins family.

Above a full-page photo of a canoodling couple, the headline read *Nero has a New Noodge*. Good for him—at his age, too. And whatever a Noodge was.

"Well?" Vronky asked over the blare of a passing ambulance siren.

"Well what?" Sophie looked closer. "He's gross. I'll give you that." An obvious non-bather. Bad spiked hair. "He's gone downhill." Tracey used to have a poster of this dude in her room back in high school. "I can't believe my sister Tracey ever worshiped at this guy's altar."

"Looks like she's still worshiping." Vronky planted her hands on her hips. "Look at the Noodge." She air-quoted Noodge.

The Noodge's head was tilted all the way back, exposing a massive tattoo taking up all the real estate on her neck and chest—a multi-colored, finely detailed rendering of Nero's unwashed hairstyle, face and blank stare. Impressive but at the same time revolting, due to the subject matter. "I bet that

3

really hurt."

"Look *closer*. Does the straw-colored hair look familiar?" Vronky lifted the limp ends of Sophie's straight blonde hair and shook them. "How about the blue eyes?" She leaned in and poked a finger onto a different picture with the Noodge's face. "Does the name Racey Hawkins ring a bell?"

"Racey? No." Hawkins, yes. The edges of the magazine wrinkled in her grip. "Just a second."

Holy cats. That wasn't … was it?

It couldn't be. "That's not Tracey. It's just a weird coincidence with a girl with a similar name." A cold wind wrapped itself around Sophie's neck, strangling her next words. "Besides, Tracey's not in New York. She's in the opposite of New York: Sugarplum Falls. With her kids. And Beau."

Beau Cabot. The name slid across her tongue like sugar and spice. It couldn't be Tracey. Tracey—had everything. *She had Beau.* Ever since Tracey was nineteen and Sophie was thirteen, Tracey had had Beau, and Beau was everything.

Well, everything Sophie had ever dreamed of: smart, kind, funny, interested in science, a good dad—probably. Not that she'd seen his fatherhood skills in action for years. Not since she was fifteen and had been disinvited from their house. Still, the qualities Beau had obviously possessed as the U.S. Air Force ROTC man in uniform who'd come to Sophie's middle school classroom for career day and swept her thirteen-year-old heart into a frenzy stood the test of time.

He's still everything. So that photo *couldn't* be of Tracey.

She pushed the magazine back at Vronky. "Probably a doppelgänger."

Vronky heaved a sigh. "How long have we known your sister? Is this *truly* out of character?"

No. No, it wasn't. But it wasn't Tracey. It was some look-alike with a made-up name. *And our shared maiden name.* "Tracey's at home in Sugarplum Falls. She's probably making holiday cookies with her kids."

Tracey didn't just have Beau Cabot, she had his two darling-amazing-perfect children. Sophie would get to have them at her place for the days after Christmas in just a few weeks. A festive-colored paper chain hung on the balcony railing at her apartment in downtown Darlington, counting down the days. It was Tracey's annual gift to Sophie: the gift of Adele and Mac.

Tracey hadn't called yet to arrange things, but surely, she hadn't changed her mind about their years-long tradition.

Who—gasp—*are named for a famous singer and a band.* Adele was for the one and only Adele. Mac went by his middle name instead of by Fleetwood, his first.

"Tracey does have a track record of rock star obsession."

Vronky cleared her throat before reading aloud in a judgy voice. "Southern-rock star Nero was seen at Madison Square Garden this weekend for the Knicks' preseason game with a new piece of candy on his arm."

"Tracey doesn't even like basketball." *But she does love rock stars.* "Besides, what lunatic would leave U.S. Air Force Captain Beau Cabot for a sleazy singer?"

For the first time, Vronky's face softened. "I've been there with you for a long time. Ever since the puffed sleeves incident."

"You mean the *flower girl is taller than the bride* incident?" Sophie's pre-teen crush on Beau was only known to Vronky, as was her pain over the indifference of the older guy who only had eyes for her more age-appropriate sister. "I still can't believe I had to wear that dress." Such puffy sleeves they'd obscured her peripheral vision. "In front of Beau." *The guy who taught me about Bernoulli's lift, the principle that kept me moving, flying all the way through graduate school.* He'd been so kind to her, even after he chose Tracey, how could her thirteen-year-old heart have relinquished him? How could her twenty-five-year-old heart not still feel some of that?

"Sophie, honey. I don't blame you for looking like someone who's just heard all pandas have gone extinct. It's a bad situation. Call Tracey and confirm, just for peace of mind. She's your sister."

"Fine. I'm dialing." Sophie stabbed the phone screen. It went to voice mail.

You've reached Racey Hawkins. Hit me up. Racey. Racey Hawkins. Proof positive that aliens had landed in her sister's soul.

Sophie went limp. Tracey had been Tracey Cabot for over a dozen years.

Beau Cabot's wife. Adele Cabot's and Mac Cabot's mother. Not Hawkins. And certainly not *Racey* Hawkins.

Good grief.

"She's changed her name." And her affections, apparently. As well as her slang. What was she, fifteen with this *hit me up* business? What did that even mean? "I seriously don't get it."

"I'm sorry I had to be the one to break it to you." Vronky's mouth pulled into a grimace. "She's messed up."

A couple of horns honked nearby, and the air smelled like car exhaust. Darlington hadn't begun to put up holiday decorations yet, at least not in this part of the city. It didn't feel like Christmas. But it would feel even *less* like Christmas for Adele and Mac. *Without a mom for Christmas.*

Worse, Beau's mother had passed away in late summer, according to a brief and almost detail-free conversation with Mom. There were a lot of those types of conversations with Mom. *Poor Beau.* Sophie's throat tightened.

She had to do something. They were her family.

"It's not a long drive to Sugarplum Falls from here." Just an hour up the highway and over the mountain pass. "I should go. Check on them and see what I can do to help. They might need me there, just for the holidays, to get them through the rough time."

"For the holidays! You, Sophie Hawkins, should *not* go up there. Not for the holidays, not even for the afternoon. This is a phone call situation at *most*." Vronky stuffed the magazine into her big purse with the Christmas tree in sequins on the side. "Do I need to list the reasons?"

"Adele and Mac are my niece and nephew. I'm their aunt." And the closest thing to their mom, at least in appearance, if not temperament. Never that.

Vronky was undeterred. "Should I start with the fact you'd be inserting yourself in a situation where you might not be welcome? Should I also note that you've never been invited to their home, not since you were fifteen?"

"It had to be scheduling conflicts or an oversight." For more than ten years? Fine. It was something else, but still. "It's not like I was exiled from Adele and Mac's lives." Tracey sent the kids to her for weeks at a time, so that they could have Aunt Sophie Time—and so that Tracey could have Tracey Time.

"Furthermore. It's not like Adele and Mac live alone in Sugarplum Falls. They live with their dad. Their dad is *Beau Cabot.* Your brother. Make that your brother for whom you have unresolved feelings—"

"Brother-in-law. In *law.*" Sophie should have been offering a different retort—against the idea that she had unresolved feelings for Beau.

"—while you're dating Dr. Matt Vaughn."

My boss. Matt was such a good guy. Really smart. *Really* smart. Not particularly magnetic or easy to relate to for most people, but an absolute genius. And cute in his horn-rimmed glasses. "Please. This has nothing to do with Dr. Vaughn. This wouldn't be a dating situation. This would be a stepping-in-during-an-emergency situation. I'm a mature adult, and these kids are potentially in deep emotional need right now." Especially because their grandma who lived nearby had also passed away. "I can ignore any residual feelings I might have for their dad. In fact, this could be the perfect chance to quash them once and for all."

A sharp wind cut against her skin and Sophie tightened her lab coat around herself. Definitely winter now. Winter without Christmas decorations was just bleak. Like Adele and Mac's holidays must be.

And Beau's.

"I'll think about your advice."

"Be careful, Sophie." Vronky took the magazine back out and waved it. "This is a mess, but you don't have to fix it."

Vronky hugged her goodbye.

Sophie went home to pack. Did Mom and Dad even know about this? If so, they would have told Sophie, right? *Maybe.*

In thoughtless haste, Sophie shoved her tote full of random, shapeless sweatshirts and sweats, the only things still clean since tomorrow should be laundry day, and then she dialed Mom. Without even offering her usual greetings, she launched. "Were you aware Tracey has lost her mind?"

Yeah, Mom had seen the article, but she also knew other aspects not named in the article, including details of Tracey's summer divorce from Beau.

"Divorce!" The word was like a lightning bolt.

"It was final in June. Didn't I tell you? Oh, maybe not."

"Mom." Geez!

"Well, Tracey insisted. You know your sister. When she gets an idea in her head, she's pretty unstoppable."

"Was this Nero person the idea in her head?"

"He's very famous."

So was Genghis Khan, and he probably had better table manners than this Nero dude.

"You knew and didn't tell me any of this?" As family, Sophie ought to be informed about important things like marital status of her only sibling.

"Of course I knew, dear. She came to your dad and me for some spending cash before she left for the concert tour. We had no choice."

What! "You're saying you provided her with cash to be a groupie?" Sophie pressed her forehead against her bedroom wall.

"Well, she knows him personally, so I wouldn't call her a groupie, per se. It does seem like her dream is coming true. She's admired him ever since he sang 'Corn Fed.' That song really swept her off her feet." Mom sighed as if this was a good thing. "Christmas wish list complete for one of my daughters."

What planet was Mom on? "What about Adele? And Mac?" And Beau?

"Beau called to see if I knew anyone who could help out with them, but I'm pretty swamped here, you know. Mrs. Ogilvie is turning ninety on Christmas Eve."

Since Mom was Mrs. Ogilvie's sole caregiver, it made sense that Mom couldn't abandon her to take care of a seven-year-old and a nine-year-old, especially kids as precocious and energetic as Adele and Mac. Heck, Mom had run out of parenting energy by the time Sophie was nine or ten—it had all been sapped by Tracey's teenage antics.

"So, Beau asked for help." *I knew it.*

"Oh, that was weeks ago. I'm sure he's found someone by now. I know he was looking for a nanny."

Adele and Mac with a nanny? No! This just got worse and worse. No nanny could have fun with, *and be patient with*, and love them like Sophie.

Clearly, they couldn't be stuck with a nanny. Certainly not for Christmastime.

She hung up. Then, without even taking time to shower or put on makeup or change out of her scrubs or pull her hair out of her nasty ponytail, Sophie threw her tote bag and all the gifts for them she'd collected so far into the back seat of her car and headed toward the mountain pass that separated Darlington from Sugarplum Falls.

Toward Sugarplum Falls, with its waterfall and its white clapboard churches, with its charm and Christmastime cheer—such a contrast to dingy, exhaust-fume-filled Darlington.

Toward Adele and Mac.

And Beau.

I only hope Beau won't turn me away.

Chapter 2

Beau

"Gemma. Why aren't you watching Mac and Adele?" Beau stood in his Air Force Reserve captain's uniform, steam clinging to his lungs, as the young woman he'd assumed would be minding his children circled the natural hot springs pool on the ground level of his home, Turtledove Place. "Where are they?"

Gemma swam her way to the edge and looked up at him with wanton eyes. "They're playing a game. I thought you'd be glad to meet me here, since you're tired from work." She shook her red hair and batted her wet lashes at him in the dim, steamy room.

He was tired from work, but he had another job to go to—right now. "I'm late for my military assignment. The kids need dinner." The first weekend of every month, he was committed to the Reserve, and he'd never been late.

"Come on, Beau. You can't be a workaholic and a daddy *all* the time. Sometimes you've gotta be a man, too." She hoisted her lean figure from the pool, wrapped herself in a towel, and stalked toward him.

"Gemma." Beau backed away from the dripping-wet girl who came at him with that same predatory look as her predecessors. Not all had been as scantily clad as this one, but they'd all sooner or later made advances on him. Gemma acted sooner. *Three weeks. She worked fast.*

"Yes, Beau?" She dropped her towel. "The kids are totally occupied. Wouldn't you like to be occupied as well?"

Beau had places to be. And none of them were in the arms of a vapid culinary school dropout who couldn't even make boxed macaroni and cheese and who let his kids atrophy on screens all day. *About the same as my ex-wife.*

"We could take a swim first, if you want."

The clock on the wall showed he had less than fifteen minutes to get out of the house or be late to his Friday night meeting with the other officers.

They'd be expecting Captain Cabot's input, as well as his presentation on troop readiness for their unit. "Get dressed, Gemma."

"Where's the fun in that?"

This got more useless by the minute. His third nanny in five months, he was getting exhausted by the revolving door.

But Gemma was not giving in. "It's such a gorgeous house, Beau. The pool, the view, the hot, lonely guy who owns it. Everything about it is rich. We could be rich together, you know. I'd be really good at it."

Even though the ticking clock demanded that Beau leave his kids in someone's care, and even though he had nowhere else to turn, he clenched his teeth and uttered the defeating words.

"Gemma, you're fired."

"Fired!" the redhead gasped, touching her bare collarbone. "But Beau, I thought …" She gathered the towel up from the deck. "I thought you hired me for *all* the reasons. Not just for the kids."

"Nope. Goodbye."

Her lower lip shot out. She wrapped the towel around herself and stomped up the stairs toward the nanny quarters on the main floor.

Without Gemma to watch Mac and Adele, he wasn't going to be able to leave for his weekend assignment at the Command Base two hours away from Sugarplum Falls.

Beau rubbed the persistent knot at the top of his spine near his right shoulder. Was there a word in the English language for how tired this year left him? At least it was almost over. If he could just get through December. Most years, December meant holidays. Not this year. This year, it meant his entire weekday career's existence hung in the balance with the survival or death of Tazewell Solutions.

With slow, plodding steps, he climbed the back stairs to his home office on the main floor, where he stayed until he heard Gemma's door slam and her car drive off. He'd have to call them at the base and tell them about his family emergency. *I've never missed a single month's assignment since I transferred from active duty to the Reserve.*

And he shouldn't now, either. There had to be a solution.

Giggles and upbeat music sailed through the air from the living room where the kids were, sure enough, playing a video game.

"Mac, Adele. You want to go see Aunt Elaine?" His late step-father's sister worked with Beau at Tazewell Solutions. Once or twice since Tracey left, Elaine had defended the home front for Beau. "She might want company for the weekend."

Mac and Adele looked up from the video game they'd become far too expert at over the past weeks of Gemma's oversight. If Aunt Elaine was in charge, she'd military-school them right out of video-game mode. Actually, Beau should have been able to do that himself, if only he'd possessed an iota of energy.

"Aw, do we have to?" Mac whined. "She doesn't like us to come over." Was his lisp getting more pronounced? The whine definitely was.

"Yeah, I broke that glass thing last time." Adele was looking at the game again. "She said I couldn't come back until I had learned some manners." Suddenly, she did look up. "Manners. M-a-n-n-e-r-s. I'm the class representative for the spelling bee right before Christmas break." She beamed. Her teeth were too big for her face, and it made her really cute. Her white-blonde hair was just like her mother's. So was Mac's.

Plus, she had a point. Elaine, at sixty, had a very low tolerance level for kid antics. He video dialed her anyway. What choice did he have?

"Elaine. Any chance you'd like to spend the weekend at Turtledove Place?" That, at least, was better than letting the kids wreck her house.

"Beau?" A loud motor wound down in the background. Probably her blender. She was the queen of green smoothies. "You didn't fire your nanny again, did you?"

"She invited me for a swim. Et cetera." The girl might as well have had dollar-signs tattooed on her eyelids.

The whirring sound ended. "That's three since August." She sipped a green smoothie on the screen.

Don't remind me. "Do you have any suggestions for a replacement n-a-n-n-y?"

Adele's head popped up from the game again. "Dad. I'm in the third grade. I can spell *nanny*. I can also spell *dulcimer* and *abstinence,* in case you're interested."

Over the video call screen Elaine raised a brow. "I'm glad they're teaching abstinence in schools these days."

"What's abstinence?" Mac shouted at Beau, shaking his game controller above his head. "Is it better than Santa Claus's aerodynamic sleigh?"

"I can also spell *havoc,*" Adele announced. "That's what Giselle said we wreaked."

"You need help, Beau."

Gemma, Giselle, Gigi. They'd been no help at all.

"Give me the weekend and I'll have someone permanent." Probably. Why did his clothes suddenly feel like they were lined with lead? "Are there any elderly widows in the Sugarplum Falls Historical Society who'd like to earn a little extra money?" He hadn't searched for help from anyone in that age range yet.

"Good nannies are hard to come by. What you need is a wife." Elaine picked up the tall glass of dark green liquid. "What about that nice Olympia Barron? She's single and attractive. On the bombshell side, if you ask me. Besides, she's on the Tazewell board of directors with us. If you showed the least hint of interest, I'm sure—"

He shook his head and angled the phone to show her that the kids were in the room. Beau was not going to discuss dating options in front of Mac and Adele.

She cupped a hand over her mouth. "Sorry," she whispered. "Fine. I wish I could help you out, but this weekend I'm swamped with a work deadline for the application submission, and next weekend I'm already committed to helping the mayor's committee for the festival."

Well, it wasn't like he could switch his assigned weekend anyway. His whole Reserve unit would be gathered for training beginning in the morning at oh-dark-thirty. "Festival?"

"All the hot chocolate you can drink."

Didn't family come before festivals? Yes, but Mayor Lisa Lang wouldn't see it that way. Beau knew better than to request that anyone, even Elaine

Tazewell, lock horns with the formidable Lisa Lang.

"Sorry, Beau. But how about this? I'll ask around at the mayor's committee when we meet next."

But he needed a solution in the next half an hour.

They hung up.

Blipping and carnival music of the video game bounced through the room. Beau leaned against the kitchen counter, which still displayed Mom's salt and pepper shakers shaped like little doves. It felt strange to be living here at Turtledove Place, Mom's house—which had been Grandma's house that Grandpa had so lovingly built for her sixty years ago—but without a wife to make it feel like a home. Not that Tracey had been great at homemaking. But still. There'd been a mother *figure* if nothing else.

It had only made sense to move in when Mom died and Beau inherited it, since in the divorce decree Tracey had gotten the house and Beau had gotten the kids.

What Beau should have gotten was a better lawyer.

Maybe he'd been trying to do anything he could to appease her, help her change her mind for the kids' sake. However, within a couple of weeks, she'd visited a tattoo artist and hopped on a rock star's tour bus. Now, she was too busy changing her name and making appearances in glossy tabloid magazines on the arm of that skinny, scraggly musician to even call home on Mac's birthday last month.

Yeah, he'd picked a real winner as the mother of his kids.

Worse, having kids hadn't saved his marriage like he'd hoped. If Mac and Adele couldn't convince Tracey to stay, nothing could. Those kids were golden.

"Daddy?" Mac raced into the room. "Can you help me sing the song for my Christmas program? It's 'Frosty the Snowman.' But I can't remember the words."

Sing?

Uh, Beau couldn't …

"Mac." Adele marched in, hands on hips. "I'll help you with the song. Leave Daddy alone." She steered him out of the room and toward the dusty piano, where she played a few notes. Not well. "You know Daddy isn't going to sing with you," she stage-whispered. "Don't ask him that. It makes him sad."

Mac shot him a look, but then started up on the lyrics about the old silk hat they found.

With an ache in his muscle at his shoulder, Beau lit a fire in the grate, and then he undid the top button on his light blue uniform shirt and pulled the captain's hat off his head. Might as well give up and call the unit commander's office, tell them he wouldn't make it this weekend.

He'd better find a new nanny. And not one with a libido set to high, and an intelligence level set to nil. Someone with principles. Someone who might learn to actually *love* Adele and Mac.

And fast. Because Beau had pressures of his own. What he hadn't discussed with Aunt Elaine was that if Tazewell *did* get awarded this military contract for the aerial surveillance software they'd been creating and investing in for the past several years, they were set for the foreseeable future. And if *not*, Tazewell Solutions wouldn't live to see another Christmas.

It might not even make payroll to the end of the year.

He pressed the commander's contact and the first ring buzzed.

At the same moment, the doorbell also rang, playing its long, old-fashioned chimes.

The door! It had to be Elaine! She'd changed her mind and decided to work on the application deadlines remotely while she watched Mac and Adele. Beau ended the call, lurched from the couch and jogged to the door. He swung it wide. "Thank you, E—"

The words died, choked off by horror. In the porch light, in a bulky parka and with a large tote bag on her shoulder, stood … "Tracey?"

Chapter 3

Sophie

It was nearly dark, though not that late. The sun set early this time of year, especially in the mountain valleys like those between Darlington and Sugarplum Falls, and Sophie had been driving a while.

At last, she made it into the town limits. She turned onto Orchard Avenue, passing what had to be hundreds of acres of fruit trees in regular lines. None bore fruit this time of year, but surely when spring came, they'd be a rage of blossoming splendor. A streetlight blinked red then green ahead, and a large, festive-looking sign welcomed her. *Sugarplum Falls. The Sweetest Little Town on Earth.*

Oh, it was even more charming than she remembered from visiting here years ago, and every little shop called to her. A huge, lit and decorated tree graced the circle drive in front of the recreation center. Every store window had lights and garlands and Christmas décor. Even the streetlights had a wreath and a bow on every pole.

A person could die of the charm.

But Sophie had a task: locate Adele and Mac.

First, she tried Tracey and Beau's address on Hill Street, where Sophie had been sending the kids' birthday gifts, but new owners said they'd lived there since summer—that they'd heard about the previous couple divorcing— and they didn't know anything else. Next, she drove through a couple of other residential neighborhoods in Sugarplum Falls, as though Beau's name would appear on a mailbox or something. It didn't. She would have to be more aggressive or creative in her search, since Beau's home address didn't show up online anywhere.

It was crazy that she didn't even know where her sister's kids lived!

Mac, Adele, where are you?

Duh. This wasn't Darlington. She could ask someone. A place like

Sugarplum Falls, people knew people. Sophie passed Sugarbabies Bakery, a sporting goods store called Sugarplum Sports, and an Italian restaurant before settling on where to stop to ask for help—Angels Landing Bookstore. Yeah, perfect. A bookstore usually employed people who knew the town and everyone in it.

Sure enough, a sweet retiree couple named Mr. and Mrs. Milliken were more than happy to help.

"Beau Cabot. Great guy." Mr. Milliken stroked his chin. "Running his late stepdad's company. Shame about his wife." He shook his head. "You look a little like her."

"Do you know where he is? I stopped by his old place, and they didn't know him."

"Yeah, yeah, of course. Nowadays he's moved up on the hill to his mom's old house. His grandma's before that, I believe. Enjoying the view from Turtledove Place." Mr. Milliken then launched into a rambling history of the hills overlooking Sugar Lake. "Head up Orchard Avenue, and hang a right at the first steep hill. You can't miss it."

It turned out Sophie could miss it. In fact, she missed it four times before finally locating the long, tree-lined driveway of Turtledove Place, even though it sported a beautiful iron gate proclaiming *Turtledove Place* over the entrance from the road.

Still, this was the place.

Sophie headed up the drive, her fingers gripping the wheel tighter with each revolution of her tires over the powdery snow. Along the front fence spaced at even intervals were decorative pairs of ironwork turtledoves. What a beautiful property. Whoa, but an even more stunning house. Light poured from all the windows of the two-story home, making it look alive and warm.

This is where Beau lives? Smoke puffed from the chimney.

Uh-oh. It had a fireplace. That might not be good. Fireplaces and Sophie shouldn't mix.

She slowed her car further as Vronky's arguments zipped around in her mind, eating away at any confidence she'd had when she left home on this big, unsolicited rescue mission.

Would Beau even want Sophie there? He hadn't invited her to his house since she was a kid, and he hadn't invited her today. The fact was, Sophie might ring the doorbell, come face to face with Beau Cabot for the first time in forever, and get shooed off the property like some kind of mangy varmint.

Her gaze slid downward to her attire. Ew. She just might be a mangy varmint, come to think of it. Was that a mustard stain on the thigh of her scrubs? Her ponytail had loosened, and strands of pale yellow partially obscured her vision, probably making her look even more bereft of personal grooming standards. Frankly, if Beau's upper lip didn't curl in derision when he saw her, Sophie would count it as a win.

Whatever. Adele and Mac would never care how their aunt looked! They were the only ones she wanted to impress with her presence—and she was bringing presents, the other kind, so she'd be impressive no matter what.

She parked the car. Reaching over the back seat, she snagged both her tote of clothes and the gift bag full of trinkets she'd been picking up for the kids since she saw them last summer. It was only little things like Silly Putty and Slinky toys, but a little went a long way sometimes.

Well, here went nothing.

The doorbell rang like a church's chimes. She shivered on the step, and footfalls sounded inside.

The door flew open, and any air that might have been floating around Sugarplum Falls disappeared. Or, at least Sophie couldn't catch any of it in her lungs.

Because there, bathed in warm, golden light, stood Beau Cabot. In his Air Force uniform, no less, with captain's bars on his broad shoulders. Sophie's stomach leapt in just the same way it had when she'd seen him for the first time as a pre-teen.

But then—

"Tracey?" His face warped from open to closed in a split-second. He took a hobbling step backward, his head shaking. "What are you—? On our anniversary?"

Sophie dropped her tote and her gift bag and put up her palms in the universal sign of *I come in peace.* "No, Beau. It's—"

"Aunt Sophie!" Shrieks of delight shattered the air, and Sophie was attacked at her legs and waist by her two favorite humans. They nearly toppled her backward under their loving force.

"How did you know we wanted to see you?" Adele asked.

"How did you find our house?" Mac said.

"Can you stay for a long time?" Adele wanted to know. "Say yes. Right now."

Sophie hugged each of the kids but kept her eyes trained on Beau's reaction. Sophie should have known better than to crash his house on his anniversary—the first one as a single man.

"Daddy, isn't it great to see Aunt Sophie?" Adele dragged Sophie—who grabbed her bags—into the warm house by the hand, pulling her from the foyer in next to the fireplace. "S-o-p-h-i-e C-a-b-o-t."

Her neck turned to fire. "You mean Hawkins, Adele. H-a-w-k-i-n-s. Like Grandma and Grandpa's last names." *And Tracey-Racey's now, apparently.*

Adele spelled it three times as the kids danced on the fireplace hearth.

Beau gazed at her, but his face was pale, as if he were looking at some kind of plague-carrier brought into his home.

I knew it. He is disgusted at the sight of me. This proves he's the one who didn't want me in his house all these years. Still, she should explain, and then figure out how to leave gracefully without hurting the kids' feelings. "I'm sorry I didn't call before I came. I didn't have your number, and I only learned today about my sister's abdication."

"You saw the article, I take it." Beau's green-around-the-gills coloring faded slightly, but it was replaced by a deep frown. He looked so different when he frowned, and from the looks of the deep lines it caused, he'd been using the expression a lot lately.

"A-b-d-i-c-a-t-i-o-n." Adele beamed, but Mac whacked her on the side of the head.

"Quit acting like a know-it-all. It's irritating. E-a-r ..."

"That's not how you spell irritating, Mac." Adele pulled on his ear.

Sophie reached out and removed Adele's pinching fingers. "I'm so glad to see you two. Now, be nice so that I can give you some little presents, *and* so

I'll want to stay longer than two minutes."

"You have to stay, Aunt Sophie!" Adele said, while Mac promised, "We'll be nice. What did you get for us?"

Sophie handed them the gift bag, and they dug into it.

"Stay?" Suddenly, Beau's face opened back up, and his hazel eyes widened.

"Only if it's okay with you." This was the moment of truth. "I don't want to intrude."

"Intrude! Hardly." Beau shook his head quickly, then he grabbed the tote from her grip. "I can't tell you how good your timing is. Let me take this upstairs. The nanny's quarters haven't been cleaned yet."

Adele affected her *young adult* tone. "Daddy fired Gemma today."

"Gemma is gone." Mac nodded. "For good."

Gemma must have been their nanny. Yikes. From the sound of it, the firing must have been abrupt. Chaos lingered in the air.

"Sophie?" Beau beckoned for her to follow him up the stairs but spoke to the kids. "You guys sit tight. I'll be right back."

The central staircase was broad and grand. At a landing halfway up, it split into two branches leading to the second floor. Here and there were carvings of those same doves she'd seen in the ironwork motifs outside.

Turtledoves?

"I hope upstairs is okay with you; it's where the family sleeps." Beau led her past several doors. "There are seven bedrooms in the house, way more than we're using. Mac and Adele share."

Seven bedrooms. Whoa. "Anywhere is fine. I'd be fine on a couch." She shoved her hair back. Great. More had fallen out of the ponytail and into her face. "It's so cool of you to let me stay."

"Let you?" Beau shook his head. "You don't understand. I was about to miss my weekend Air Force Reserve assignment for the first time in the eight years since I left active duty."

"You're not on active duty now?" When Sophie had been downtown, that bookstore man, Mr. Milliken, had said something about Beau changing jobs. "Reserve instead?" Reserve seemed like a big change for a guy who'd been on active duty. Now to only spend one weekend a month? Of course, it was hard to imagine Beau doing otherwise. He had military service in his blood.

"When Pops died, he left me at the helm of his company Tazewell Solutions." Pops—his stepdad. "It's military software development, so it made sense, plus it let me put down roots." He frowned. "Just in time, I guess." He was thinking about Tracey's exit, obviously. Then he swept the frown aside. "In time, just like you. Now I don't have to miss my Reserve assignment."

"You nearly missed it because of this Gemma person?" Sophie took off her coat, laying it on the bed and tugging at the shirt of her scrubs. Why was she suddenly feeling so exposed? Scrubs covered everything. "What happened?"

Beau rolled his eyes. "Let's just say she misread the job description. She thought the word *nanny* was spelled *m-i-s-t-r-e-s-s*. When she caught me unawares in her barely-theres after work at the pool tonight, I cut the power to her engines immediately."

A-ha. But … wait a second. What was he doing at a pool in this subzero weather? Sugarplum Falls temperatures were not for the easily chilled.

A question for another time.

"So, it would be okay if I stay for the weekend?" A question she hadn't dreamed she'd be asking Beau Cabot when she woke up this morning. Or any other morning since Tracey married him.

"Okay? It would be a miracle I hadn't had time to pray for yet." Beau exhaled loudly. "Your timing couldn't have been better." Beau's gaze brimmed with gratitude.

Gratitude was nice. But it would be nicer if something else shone there, like interest. She shouldn't wish that, obviously. Beau was her brother-in-law, and Sophie was dating Dr. Matthew Vaughn.

"Then I'll stay. Thanks for letting me in your house."

He tilted his head, questioning. "You're welcome?" For a second he searched her face, but then his question cleared. "And I mean that—you *are* welcome. In fact, it's nice to have you here. You haven't visited in a long time. I'm glad you decided to come."

What? As if she were the one who'd decided to banish herself from the

Cabot home.

Though that mystery beckoned to be unraveled, Beau looked at the glowing digital clock on the nightstand and caught his breath. "I'd better take off. I have a long drive and a report due in an officers' meeting tonight."

A report. Wow, he was under a lot of pressure, it seemed.

"Well, I'm here. Don't worry for a second about Mac and Adele."

The frown lines on his face softened, and he leaned forward and tugged her into a partial, awkward hug. Sophie stiffened. *He's hugging me.* For a split second, her heart began to race. *He's hugging me!* But the adrenaline drained instantly when he spoke.

"I'll be home Sunday night, not sure what time. Thanks so much, Sophie. I always liked you. You're a good kid." He hustled out of the bedroom and down the staircase.

Kid. A good kid. *I'm still a kid to him.* She'd always be a kid. Nothing but the kid-sister of his wife. She flopped down onto the bed, such a fool for even thinking a moment that he'd see her otherwise.

Nope.

Well, she could let herself sulk, but a niece and a nephew were waiting below—and she had gifts and fun to spread around. Instead of curling into a ball of disappointment, she tripped off down the wood floors of the hallway to the staircase. Over the banister to below, Beau was hugging each kid goodbye. He waved up to Sophie and mouthed a thank you and—break her heart in twelve pieces—blew her a kiss.

The tendons behind her knees suddenly revolted, Sophie gripped the banister. Her kneecap whacked a little carved face of a dove, its sharp beak digging into her skin.

Ouch. Blast her knees. Even if he called her a kid, Sophie wasn't one like the day she first saw him. She was twenty-five. She had a master's degree and was one exam shy of her professional license. She should not be getting weak-kneed over him anymore.

But he blew me a kiss!

***

"What's with all the bird carvings?" she asked the kids the next morning over peanut butter pancakes with banana smoothies. They'd already been on a quick trip into Sugarplum Falls proper this morning to a grocery store for milk and to the dollar store for Saturday craft-making supplies. "They look like doves."

Mac shrugged and shoveled pancake in his mouth.

Adele shrugged, too. Which was unusual. Normally the girl had an answer for everything.

"Did your grandma like doves?"

"This was our dad's grandma's house. Maybe she liked them." Adele was much more interested in the smiley face made out of chocolate syrup on top of her pancake than in conversation about décor. "Usually people call them pigeons and they don't like them then."

"Why do people love doves and hate pigeons, Aunt Sophie?" Mac asked through a stuffed mouth. Everything Mac said was at top volume, and the kid, especially with a full mouth, had a serious lisp going on.

I wonder what Beau would say if I helped Mac with that. Would I be overstepping?

Possibly. She'd wait and ask permission. Even if he'd looked at her like she walked on water when she arrived last night, Sophie's time at Turtledove Place was still purely probationary—and would determine whether she could make any return visits.

But, had Beau insinuated that she'd stayed away of her own volition? It wasn't clear.

Either way, she'd better tread softly if she wanted to be part of these kids' lives.

"Tell you what—I'll organize our afternoon crafts," Sophie said after breakfast wound up, "while you two go out and build a snowman."

"But Aunt Sophie. We don't know how to build a snowman." Mac wiggled his foot into his boot while Sophie held it still. Adele was dressing herself. "We never did it before."

"Big ball, medium ball, little ball." Sophie demonstrated with her arms. "You guys get started and I'll come out in a bit with a carrot for the nose."

"Can we use Daddy's scarf for Mr. Snowman's neck?" Adele already had it around her own neck and was tugging it dangerously tightly. "Daddy won't mind."

Nearly an hour later, they had a snowman, but not a very good one. The snow in Sugarplum Falls was more like powdered sugar than regular, packable snow. Sophie had had to bring a spray bottle of water to increase the moisture and make it stick together.

"You guys didn't do too badly for your first snowman ever." Sophie balanced her own snow hat on top of Mr. Snowman's head. "How come you haven't built any before?"

"Mommy didn't like snow." Count on Adele to put things bluntly. "And Daddy ..."

"Daddy what?" Sophie should not be pumping a child for information. It was probably unethical on some level. "Doesn't like snow either?" she prompted.

"Daddy's sad!" Mac said. Although his *sad* sounded like *thad*. Mac made a powdery snowball and tossed it at Mr. Snowman.

Beau was sad. Of course he was. "His Mom died this year," Sophie explained. "That would make him sad."

"He was thad for a while before that. A thad dad." Mac attempted another snowball, larger, and threatened to topple their creation. Quick! A distraction before the destruction.

"Hey," she said, "how about we make a Mrs. Snowman to go with our Mr. Snowman?"

Adele and Mac were both enthusiastic and began rolling the base together.

"Yeah," Adele shouted. "Then when Mrs. Snowman is there, Mr. Snowman won't be sad and tired like Dad."

Any guy in Beau's circumstances would need cheering, but the return of Mrs. Tracey Snowman-Cabot probably wasn't going to happen, and even if it did, Beau might not be happy. *Tracey is such a fool.*

Inside, Sophie set steaming mugs of hot cocoa in front of the kids, and then gave them each an ice cube to plop in and a handful of miniature marshmallows. "What do you guys have planned for Christmas traditions this year? Caroling? Decorating cookies?"

"I like cookies," Mac said, sipping and talking loudly. "What's care-ling?"

"What's caroling!" Christmas caroling to neighbors was a mandatory Hawkins family Christmas activity. "When you go singing at your friends' houses and take them cookies. Didn't your mom take you guys caroling?"

"Mom talked about it once, last year, but we didn't go." Adele shook her head and affected her adult voice again. "Dad hates singing. He wouldn't dream of singing for neighbors. Or anybody else."

"Really? But your dad has a great voice."

"Nope." Adele shook her head.

Weird. Beau used to be the guy who took his guitar everywhere, making Tracey swoon and brag. Okay, and making Sophie swoon and turn green with jealousy.

"He should sing with us." Boy, Mac had a shout on him. "If it's neighbor-singing, they won't care if it's good or bad."

Sophie chuckled. "You're not wrong, Mac. In fact, the worse the better, as long as the singing is short and ends with a plate of cookies." And it was crazy to quit singing, especially when Beau had kids. Music is key to kids' development. Singing with a dad could be formative. She'd have to talk him into it. Somehow make him see how stingy he was being with his talents.

"I like cookies," Mac said again. "Can we make some?"

Sophie already had a full slate of activities planned for this too-short weekend. "We'll have to see. Maybe next time." *If there is a next time.*

"I like cookies." Mac was a broken record. "And hot chocolate. I could drink all of Sugar River if it was made of hot chocolate. I could drink all the hot chocolate at the Hot Chocolate Festival, but they won't let me."

"There's a festival? Dedicated to hot chocolate?" That was a celebration Sophie could get behind. Hot cocoa was one of life's greatest pleasures. Especially in front of a fire. *But no fireplaces for me. Nope.*

"Yeah. I think it's soon." Adele left for a minute and came back with her backpack. From inside, she pulled a crumpled paper. "They want all the kids in the whole town to go, but we never go."

25

"Stop the presses. Have I stepped into Grinchville? No caroling, no cocoa festival?"

Mac giggled, peeking at Sophie over the rim of his mug. "I'm the grinchiest Grinch!" He growled, and some of his cocoa splashed onto the table.

"I tell you what, if it was this weekend, you and I would be *going*." Sophie stomped her foot. Alas, the party was next weekend.

Maybe I should come back.

Except … no. There'd be someone else caring for the kids full time by then, surely. "Who's going to be your next nanny?" she asked without thinking about the fact she was only there out of Beau's desperation.

"We don't want a nanny. We want a mommy." Mac slurped the dregs of his cocoa. "Can I have some more?"

A mommy. Of course they wanted their mom to come back. It made the most sense. Even though Tracey-Racey was too busy living out her teenage dream to act like their mom for now, of course they held out hope that she'd come to her senses and return soon.

Who could blame them? *Mac and Adele deserve an intact family.*

So did Beau.

***

Saturday flew past with hide and seek, races down the stairs, and crafts. Sunday was morning at a nearby church, followed by board games and a Christmas music dance-off. To appease Mac's begging sweet tooth, they even baked a batch of cupcakes from a mix, but there wasn't time for cookies from scratch, which meant no singing to the neighbors.

Dang it. Sophie would leave in the morning *without* caroling, or making Mac's cookies, or even decorating the house for Christmas.

How were Mac and Adele going to have a semblance of a real Christmas without a mom—and with their *thad dad* obviously running on empty?

Sunday night at bedtime, Sophie supervised their baths, and then they gathered around the fireplace for a story and brushing tangles from Adele's freshly washed hair. Her time with them was basically over.

"Good night, Adele." Sophie hugged her nine-year-old niece. "You're my favorite niece."

"What about me?" Mac stomped his foot in his railroad train pajamas. "I thought I was your favorite, Aunt Thophie."

"You're my favorite nephew."

"What are we going to do together tomorrow night?" Adele's eyes were bright with anticipation. "I bet we could get Daddy to choose us a tree to cut down. *That's* our Christmas tradition."

"Who's talking about Christmas traditions?" a man's voice hollered from the kitchen, and the door to the garage clunked shut.

"Daddy!" Adele and Mac abandoned Sophie and rushed to hug Beau.

He looked tired but not sad. At least there was that.

"Thanks, Sophie. I'll put them to bed, since it's late." He talked to the kids, rubbed their heads, and then took them upstairs to tuck them into bed.

Bummer. Sophie had wanted one last bedtime with the kids. *I don't know when I'll see them again.*

Instead, she started the dishes in the kitchen, trying as hard as she could to not think about how fine that man looked in his uniform, even after a long weekend of work.

Rumpled Captain Cabot was almost as good as sharp and clean Captain Cabot.

A dozen colored plastic cups and cocoa mugs later, she felt a presence at her side and looked up to see Beau, showered and changed out of uniform into jeans and a t-shirt. The sleeves were tight across his biceps.

"Hey, Sophie." He picked up a dishtowel and began pulling cups off the rack, drying them, and then putting them in the cupboard, comfortable, like they did this together every day. "It's really coming down out there. Serious blizzard status. Bad roads in the canyons or I would have been home an hour earlier to help get the kids ready for bed."

"I didn't mind." While she washed and he dried a few more dishes, Sophie gave him the report on their weekend's activities, as if she was the pre-teen babysitter and he was the adult father of the kids asking for a detailed account of the time spent. Sadly, the moment bore no relation to the sparking electricity she'd been secretly dreaming of between Beau and herself if only he'd met her as an adult and not a middle-school kid.

27

"How was your assignment this weekend?"

"Not bad." He half-shrugged. "It's a great second job."

If he'd become a pilot, Tracey would have bragged it up, so he must have a different job. "What are you doing there? Readiness training? Load planning? Air mobility support?"

Beau set down Mac's *Captain Firestarter* cup and looked askance at Sophie. "How do you know the different duties of an air force unit?"

"Uh, former plane-obsessed pre-teen here." She waved a hand up and down her scrubs-clad frame. "No, I don't still have posters of World War II-era planes, but I've got all the designs memorized up here." She pointed at her temple. "I could totally be a plane spotter."

Slowly, Beau started to nod. "We did initially bond over airplanes, didn't we?"

Sophie's heart looped-the-loop, like a vintage biplane in an air show. "I was the kid with braces on the front row who wouldn't put her hand down when you and the other ROTC guys came to our class on career day. I'm afraid I may have gone on a little too long about the P-36 Hawk clad with enough gorgeous chrome to blind an enemy pilot."

"I remember that." Beau nodded. "I was surprised you'd heard of the P-36. That's a good little spitfire of a bird."

"Confession—I assumed you were all pilots already, and that you trained in vintage planes."

"You definitely made an impression." Suddenly, his face clouded. "If not, I probably wouldn't have stopped your sister in the hallway to get her number that day after the presentation." Friday night's frown lines returned, deep ravines.

Sophie retraced the past. If Beau hadn't come to Sophie's class to explain ROTC and the Air Force to them. If Beau hadn't stayed a little longer to answer Sophie's questions. If Tracey hadn't come to pick up Sophie midday for her orthodontist appointment. If Tracey hadn't flirted with him so mercilessly.

All the ifs.

If only. Then, Beau wouldn't be the *thad dad.*

Geez. Tracey hadn't known a B-1 bomber from a crop duster. How could Beau have been fooled by her act?

Now Sophie was frowning, too, but she said, "If not, we wouldn't have Mac and Adele, and I'd never trade them for anything."

Beau searched Sophie's face. "Can I ask you something?" he said. "What are you doing for the rest of the week?"

Chapter 4

Beau

He might have been way out of line, throwing out a job offer to his sister-in-law. He'd spent less than five minutes conversing with her in the past dozen years, and yet he asked her to become the caretaker of his children full time? With Gigi and Gemma and Giselle, he'd required extensive interviews, and application forms, and references, and—

And where had that gotten him?

She turned off the water in the sink. The dishes were done. "Are you saying you don't have child-care lined up for tomorrow?"

"Or the day after. Or any other day."

Sophie frowned. Her eyebrows pushed together in a different way from how Tracey's did. When Tracey pushed her brows together, it was usually in anger. Sophie's way looked thoughtful, as if his question really troubled her. "We should probably talk options. Maybe we should sit down or something."

"Good idea." They walked into the living room, and the grandfather clock chimed nine. A few pine boughs graced the mantel. "Did you put these here? They smell really good."

"I hope it's okay, but I lopped them from one of the trees in the side yard."

"Totally fine. Turtledove Place has plenty more where that came from. The whole back acreage is forestland."

"*Acreage?* Of forest?"

Oh, dear. She wasn't another one of those women, was she? Not Sophie, too. The knot at his shoulders tightened.

"It's a big place. Probably too much for just me and the kids. I might downsize." It might be callous to test her this way. "Or donate it to be a boys ranch or something."

Beau eyed her carefully. How she reacted would tell him a lot.

"Would you work it out that you could still choose a Christmas tree from it?"

Christmas tree. She was regretting the loss of a tree. The knot in his shoulder loosened a tiny fraction, and he mumbled something about guessing he could put that in a clause.

"Adele and Mac are really looking forward to getting a tree with you. It's tradition, they said."

Beau had walked in on that conversation. "I hadn't really planned it out."

"That's what Christmas is, to your kids," she said.

Beau's heart lurched. "I hadn't—" Christmas. Right. Since Mom died, he hadn't let the fact it was Christmas sink in. "I mean, the kids won't really notice if we downplay the holidays just for one year."

Sophie gave him a look that said *you're not being serious.* For a second, he withered under it, until she finally spoke, but it wasn't the accusation about his lazy fathering he'd expected. Instead, she said, "You've had a rough year, Beau."

That was putting it mildly.

"But so have they."

Sure. Of course.

"They lost their mom."

As had Beau. Plus his wife.

Oh … but *they* had lost *their* mom, too. Beau clutched the mantel. His fingers flexed on the wood.

"Yeah," Sophie whispered. She obviously had seen something dawn on his face. "They feel what you feel, so you understand them."

Beau sank into one of the recliners near the fireplace.

Sophie planted herself on the armrest of the sofa, perching like a little white bird to watch over him.

But she was right, and he had to do something, and the words were out before the idea was fully formed. "I need to give them Christmas," he said. This year, more than ever before. "They need Christmas." And not just the stash of toys he'd ordered online on Black Friday, adding the gift-wrapping option, and stashed in his closet upstairs. That wasn't enough.

"If you ask me, both of those statements are equally true."

Beau looked up at Sophie. He did need to give. And they did need to receive. For someone so young, she was right really often today.

The problem was that as a kid, Beau had always equated Christmas with childhood wonder. Mom made sure of it, even when Dad was being ... Dad. But today, not one drop of wonder remained in his cup.

"So." He met her gaze. My goodness, her eyes were a pale, ice-blue. Different from Tracey's. Soul-penetrating. Like a lark's song on a cold morning. "To give them Christmas. What do I do?"

"Besides cutting down the tree? Whatever you want to do." She reached for his forearm. A soft tingling radiated from her gentle touch. Comfort. Peace. Unfamiliar, but welcome. "The kids adore you. I'm sure it's hard, but you're doing it well."

Ha. "When Tracey left, for a couple of months at least I had my mom to lean on, and then"—he stifled a groan with a hard gulp—"who gets pneumonia in the summer?"

Sophie blinked at him. "Oh, Beau."

Her tender words combined with her touch, and Beau found himself saying more. "They did everything they could for her, but she didn't rally. She missed my stepdad so much that she said she wasn't sorry to go." He grimaced. "Am I wrong? Shouldn't she be sorry?"

"She should. I'm sure she would miss you and the kids." She spoke softly.

"Not enough, though." His voice went into a hoarse whisper. "Not enough to rally and stay."

He gazed at Sophie. Her face was all softness, but without pity. More like admiration. He didn't deserve admiration.

Since Mom died, everyone always asked Beau how he was doing. All his replies were lies: *Doing well. Hanging in, thanks.* Now, however, twenty minutes with Sophie, and he was a fire hydrant of emotion.

He twisted the cover and slowed the flow before his voice cracked or moisture could gather in his eyes. "So, what do you think? Can you stay in Sugarplum Falls?"

32

Sophie sighed and moved her hand from his arm, leaving a warm patch. It'd been a long time since he'd been touched like that. Tenderly.

"I'm not sure. Of course, Adele and Mac are everything to me, but—"

He rubbed his eyes. "I get it. Adele said you're studying like a board? I don't really know what that means. Sorry."

Sophie's laugh stirred a happiness at the back of his chest, like a sudden wind picked up a flurry of powder snow. "I think she meant my boards to receive my speech therapy certification. I take it sometime soon, by the end of the year. Then I'll be licensed and can practice full time."

"Speech therapy? I didn't know you were studying that." Boy, if any kid could use speech therapy, it was Mac. Beau had assumed the lisp would go away on its own by now, but it hadn't. "Bet you'd be good at it." Kids loved her, at least his kids did. It was always Aunt Sophie this and Aunt Sophie that after they came home from visits to her house—and begging to see her when she wasn't around.

"Actually, I think I am good at it. Not bragging." Pink blossomed across her porcelain skin, making her look pretty, at least in a modest-maiden way. "I love it. I love kids. And since I don't have any now, and don't know when or if I'll get to have my own, it's a great way to spend time with them."

"You've always got Mac and Adele." As in now. "Anytime you want."

Her face and voice flattened. "I haven't been invited to that often."

But, she was the one who refused to set foot in his house all these years. What was she saying? "You're invited now."

She blinked at him a few times. "Thanks." Half her mouth smiled. Sort of.

Her *not invited often* statement resonated. She'd never visited, for what, over a decade? And yet she had kept in touch with Tracey. Beau had always figured he must have offended her somehow. It was the only thing that made sense.

Luckily, though, she'd set that aside and come in his hour of greatest need. He owed her big thanks.

"I just appreciate what you've done for me already. You'd better get back to studying. And work, if you're working while going to school."

Where was he going to dig up child-care beginning, oh, eighteen hours from now when the kids got off the bus from school? This really was not a great time for Beau to be ditching out of Tazewell Solutions early every afternoon to go hang out at home. So many details pressed on him at work, everything from confirming hiring of that Kingston guy as new legal staff to the all-important U.S. Department of Defense contract application. That deadline loomed, and the government was supposedly fast-tracking announcing it by the end of the year.

Beau had to finish it, but he was mentally blocked.

He dragged out a sigh.

"Yeah, work," she said. "I do have a job at Darlington Speech Clinic."

Beau had looked into that clinic for special help one time, when he'd had his stuff together and Mac's speech had come to the forefront of his mind. Then things had fallen apart again, and he hadn't followed through.

"I'm still an intern and don't have official clients yet, but I'm on the schedule. Dr. Vaughn does count on me." From the look on her face, the wheels of her mind were spinning. "I do need good references."

That made sense. "You have responsibilities there."

Then again, all her statements sounded like she was trying to talk herself into going back to work, instead of talking herself into staying with Mac and Adele. *She seems torn.*

"Don't worry about us. I mean, unless you'd *like* to stay."

"I do want to stay. Believe me. But I still have a lot of studying to do, as well."

"If studying is the main concern, the kids do have school all day." Maybe he shouldn't press. But the truth was, if Sophie stayed, so many of Beau's worries would just go away. They loved her, did what she said, and she was nothing like Gemma or Giselle or Gigi. None of that pawing, hungry look from her. Sophie had touched him, but in a nourishing, not flirtatious, way.

He wouldn't have to worry about Sophie chasing after or falling for him.

"I do love them, Beau. I wish I could be here with you to give them their best Christmas ever."

"Best ever?" Ha. Hard to picture. "I'd probably aim lower, as in *not the*

34

most horrible Christmas ever as my goal instead." Frankly, with every single job at Tazewell Solutions riding on Beau right now, he probably didn't have it in him to make a childhood-wonder Christmas, like Mom always created. He definitely didn't have enough of his old energy to do that. For now, he was working under the new normal of survival as the top goal.

"You're frowning again." Sophie reached out and laid a light finger on his knee, and it warmed him again. But, what was that tingle, too? Nothing. It wasn't anything.

He mustered feigned enthusiasm. "Best ever!" He raised a triumphant fist and let it drop slowly. "At least I'll try. For their sake."

"Thanks, Beau. I know it's hard." Sophie rose from her perch on the armrest of the sofa and stood in front of him. "I should head back in the morning. I'll do what I can at work, and see about scheduling time to come back. At the very least, I could come next weekend."

"You'd come back?" A glimmer of hope shone.

"I hear there's a hot chocolate festival, and Mac begged to go. If I can't help out during the week, maybe I can at least help you give them Christmas."

It was only a fractional solution, but Sophie was the one person he could count on to inject real Christmas into his kids' lives. "Beggars can't be choosers, and I'll take everything from you I can get."

For a split second, Sophie's eyes widened. She moistened her lips. They were really pink now, setting off her creamy skin.

"I do love them." Her voice was a sweetness-laced whisper, and for a second, he misheard the words as *I do love you* and his insides reflex-startled.

Beau shook himself. "Huh?" His senses reset when his mind replayed the sounds as *I do love them.* Duh, of course Sophie loved them. *That was a weird reaction.*

"Me, too," he said, recovering his composure. "I love them so I want what's best for them. A caregiver who loves them is best for them." Which, obviously, wouldn't be any recycled version of Gemma.

The truth was, he either needed Sophie, or else—as Aunt Elaine suggested—he was going to have to find a wife.

Sophie had work and school and a life. Which meant the only longer-term solution was Beau had to find a wife.

An image of the undulating figure of Olympia Barron pacing toward him popped into his mind. A wife. As in one with all the wifely benefits. Not the worst prospect, especially considering the glacial way Tracey had treated Beau more or less since Mac was born.

"Good night, Beau." Sophie reached out and pressed his hand. "It's going to work out. I promise. You've got this."

Not alone, he didn't. Not at all.

Chapter 5

Sophie

In the dim of her bedroom, just three doors down from the freshly washed, heavenly clean-scented Beau Cabot, Sophie pulled herself into the tightest ball she could become under the white goose-down comforter on the bed.

Oh, he was so beautiful, and so broken, and she hadn't loved him this much before, even as an impetuous teenager. The ache spread from her heart to her belly to her entire chest cavity. If only she could soothe his pain, make him feel whole again.

That man in the room down the hall was *not* the real Beau Cabot. Instead, there remained a shell of his former self, and of what he could and should be. When he'd talked about his mother's death, it had killed Sophie a little inside. How was he even surviving?

Tracey! That villainess! She'd done this to Beau. If she were here right now Sophie would tie her to a chair and give her a really bad perm that left her with split ends that frizzed and made her head look like a Tesla coil.

She lay back and stared at the ceiling. She had to help him find himself again—and not lose the kids in the process.

Truly, there was no one else to do it.

She pulled out her phone. Yep, a bunch of texts from Vronky, all pumping Sophie for information about Beau.

He's still Beau. Well, mostly. *Smart. Handsome. Kind—but in a military officer way.*

Vronky's response popped up immediately. *You know I mean how IS he? Like, is he emotionally available? Are you going to take a chance and flirt with him finally?*

Sophie shut off her phone.

If only she could stay longer at Turtledove Place, be in their lives daily for a while, something told her she could not only help the kids, she could also set things right for Beau, make him remember who he used to be—and show him how to be that person again.

Pshaw, right. She sat up and leaned against the headboard. What made her, someone he thought of as a kid-sister, believe she'd have any influence over him? She was just being the same ridiculous dreamer she'd always been when it came to Beau Cabot.

Even when she'd ventured to flirt with him by touching his arm, his knee, he'd shown zero reaction. He wasn't interested in Sophie at all, other than as his children's aunt and babysitter. She squeezed her eyes shut. *Go to sleep— and stop dreaming.*

Before daylight, a pounding awakened Sophie. She shot up in bed, taking a second to get her bearings. Right. She was in Sugarplum Falls, at Beau's house, and it was Monday morning. She rubbed her eyes and pulled her hair into place.

More pounding accompanied a little squeaky voice. "Aunt Sophie!" Adele said. "Are you awake?"

I am now. She tugged her sweatshirt down and blinked a few times to reset her brain. "Come on in, sweetie."

Adele burst through the door. "School's canceled! We get to stay home with you!"

Uh, right. Adele wished. "That's a sweet idea, but it's no use. I really do have to leave, and you and Mac need to get ready for school." Sophie dragged herself out of bed. "Do you want me to braid your hair and loop it with bows? We could do Christmas bows. It would be festive."

"Aren't you listening? There's too much snow, and they canceled school. I heard it on Daddy's old-fashioned radio."

But Sophie had to get back to work on the other side of the mountain pass. "Are you sure?"

Beau appeared at Sophie's bedroom door. He was still in yesterday's t-shirt and jeans, rumpled, as if he'd slept in them. Deep lines etched down the sides of his face. "Avalanche on the mountain pass between Sugarplum Falls and Darlington. The school district announced a late start, though, not a full cancellation. We're used to dealing with snow."

"Avalanche! Was anyone hurt?" No one. Whew. Just inconvenienced. "What about Tazewell Solutions? Can you get to work today?"

He sighed. "Hilltop roads don't get plowed until long after everywhere else. As boss, though, I should still try as soon as the plows come through. We have, ahem, a big project looming."

The *ahem* made it sound really big. Sophie was dying to ask about it, but if it was military software, she probably wouldn't understand it anyway, which she knew because she'd tried and failed to interpret engineering jargon used extensively on the Tazewell Solutions website.

So she'd internet-stalked Beau. So sue her.

"Daddy, can't you stay home? Just this once?" Adele hung on his arm, batting her eyes. "Aunt Sophie said we could make cookies all together."

Not true. "I said someday we should. For Christmas caroling."

"Today is someday!" Adele danced like Clara in *The Nutcracker*, in circles around the room. "Cookies and caroling. Let's do it! I'm going to tell Mac!"

Beau looked sheepishly at Sophie. "I know I was pressuring you to stay, but I promise I didn't order the avalanche on my wish-list to Santa."

If she'd thought of it, Sophie might have.

"I'll make cookies with the kids. You have, *ahem*, work. Is it anything you can do from home?" He did have that home office off the kitchen.

"If the internet weren't down, yeah."

Wow. "Some storm."

"You probably have studying. I can watch the kids."

"Most of the material is online." Other than the one book she'd brought along. "I can study when I get home tonight."

Beau pulled a smile. "Thanks, Sophie. It's going to sound weird, but …"

"But what?"

"But it kind of feels like the universe is making you stay."

"That does sound weird." And beautiful.

"Forget I said anything." He shook himself. "Adele demands we all make cookies together. Are we on?"

They were.

Under Adele's direction, Mac was in charge of measuring. Sophie was allowed to dump ingredients into the bowl. Beau was designated the stuff-finder—ingredients, bowls, tools. When the dough was done, Sophie rolled it out to an even thickness.

Beau produced a large jar of cookie cutters, to the kids' shrieks of delight. "Adele, you choose first."

Adele chose a snowman shape to start. Mac selected a gingerbread man.

"Impressive skill." Sophie picked through the jar for a Christmas tree. "It always takes me forever to locate which drawer holds stuff I don't use often, like cookie cutters."

"It was my grandma's kitchen. I made sugar cookies with her every Christmas. Why do you think I volunteered to be the Stuff-Finder?"

If only he weren't so incredibly cute when he was having fun with his kids! Then Sophie wouldn't be tingling like this, her face and fingertips alternating hot and cold every time he brushed past.

"I'm making angels." Adele now held the angel cookie cutter. "You get to do stars." She shoved the star cutter from the jar at Mac.

"I want to do gingerbread man shapes, though." Mac frowned. Sophie really did need to help him so he wouldn't say *thaypth* instead of *shapes.* "Can't I do the gingerbread man, Aunt Sophie?"

"Of course you can." Sophie handed him the gingerbread man and took the star back for herself. "Besides, I called stars a long time ago."

Finally, all the dough was cut and arranged on the pans. While the cookies baked, the kids went up to change their clothes out of their sticky shirts and pants, and Beau washed dishes. Sophie cleaned counters, and then brushed the flour off her old sweatshirt.

"I noticed something different about you." Beau set a measuring cup in a drawer.

"You did?" Sophie startled. *Please say it's that I'm not a kid anymore.*

"Really different—at least from the other people who come to help me with the kids. It's that you haven't asked to see the house and the grounds. You're not even curious?"

Oh. That. "I've been a little swamped being Aunt Sophie. But I did have a question when you were gone, and Adele couldn't answer it."

Beau leaned against the counter. "Shoot."

"Okay, I love the name of the house, and the motifs of the doves are everywhere. It's really cool. Are they special to someone?"

For the first time, the ravines on his face softened. "Yeah, actually. Turtledoves were my grandmother's favorite bird."

She set down her bar mop and, with a pointing index finger, counted the bird motifs. "Favorite bird I can understand, but do you know there are thirty-six of them just in this room alone?"

Beau chuckled. "Sophie, you're different."

"Do you mean that in a good way? Never mind." She physically waved away the awkwardness. "Back to my question. There must be more to it than just *favorite bird*, since 'The Twelve Days of Christmas' isn't very many people's favorite holiday song." Truly, some found the repetition to be a groan-inducer.

Beau put the final spoon in the drawer and led her toward the living room. "I meant it as a compliment. You're perceptive." He stood beneath the transom between the kitchen and the living room and pointed out a tiny carving of doves she hadn't seen before. "My grandmother loved them because they're symbols of love and fidelity. They mate for life. The male helps raise the young, and they nest together. In fact, in medieval times, all love potions called for the heart of a dove."

Sophie shuddered. "Someone drank a heart?" But also … cool and sweet at the same time. "Who does that? For love, especially? And shouldn't it taste good, not like organ meats?"

For the first time since Sophie arrived, Beau gave a full smile. "No, I agree. It's nasty."

Taking her through the main floor of the house, he pointed out a couple more hidden turtledoves in the texture on the ceiling. "My grandfather built this house with my grandmother in mind, and he put everything in it she would want to have, from the top floor's views of the lake to the basement's amenities. He added the motif to show that he would be her forever love, and that he would help her raise her family in this place."

"No wonder it's such an easy place to love." Or fall in love. Further.

They headed back to the oven-warmed kitchen, and Sophie's heart was warm enough to bake cookies. Instead of doves' hearts, those medieval love doctors should have just mentioned the meaning instead.

Oh, if only love potions were a thing. A little fantasy spun out: *Sophie dipped the cup into a steaming cauldron and pulled forth the love-concoction. She handed it to Beau, and he sipped it while meeting her eyes, which instantly went from passing interest to desperate love. He swept her into his arms, pulled her close, and—*

The oven beeped that the cookies were done.

Geez. It was like she'd reversed her age by a dozen years. She had to stop fantasizing. She wasn't a teeny bopper with a crush anymore. Besides, Beau had been through too much this year to even think about getting involved with a woman. He'd fired his nanny for coming on to him. Sophie had better purge all thoughts of romance immediately.

She went to the kitchen to pull out the cookie sheet and insert the final batch to bake.

"Humph." He shoved his phone back in his pocket when she returned to where he sat in the living room next to the kids who were playing a video game. "Another storm is coming this way, and schools are out for the rest of the day, and maybe tomorrow."

Whoa. She'd called the office, and it didn't sound like Darlington was getting hit anywhere near this much by the storm. Would the clinic believe that she was really stranded by weather in Sugarplum Falls?

What would Dr. Vaughn think if he found out I'm staying with my very attractive brother-in-law, playing house?

"School's out all day, kids." Beau hustled them off the couch. "Who wants to play in the snow? I know a good game."

The kids shouted for joy and ran for their coats.

Beau turned to her. "Thanks for helping me."

"Helping *you?*"

"Yeah, helping me give the kids a better Christmas—like you said."

"We've only done cookies."

42

"Maybe, but I wouldn't have done even that much. I needed you to jumpstart me."

Jumpstart. Ha. If Beau Cabot had any idea how much he jumpstarted Sophie with every word and look, every little compliment telling her she was different, every little brush against her, he would have ejected her from Turtledove Place immediately.

She'd better shut off the faucet of interest right now.

Chapter 6

Beau

This snow day was going down as one of the more surreal days of Beau's life. First, Sophie had insisted he eat breakfast, which Beau hadn't done for far too long. And *mama mia*, she could cook. She'd made him a third fresh waffle when he finished his first two.

Then, there was the cookie project, where her main comment was how impressive it was that he knew his way around his grandma's kitchen.

The truth was, Mom hadn't moved anything when she took up residence, so after spending most of his life there and having it unchanged, it wasn't that impressive for Beau to know where the mixer and the measuring cups and the cream of tartar were.

However, it felt so good to bask in Sophie's praise. Her sister hadn't had a kind word for him in ages.

Like he'd told her, she … was different.

"You haven't seen Turtledove Place yet, or the grounds."

"I've been a little busy," she'd asserted.

Precisely. Being the world's greatest aunt. The kids hadn't been this happy in forever. Not since Mom died, and maybe even a long time before that, due to the raincloud that was Tracey's attitude hanging over them all the time. But when he'd offered her a tour of the multi-million-dollar property, Sophie asked about the doves.

Instead, he'd talked about his grandparents' epic love story. Sophie had sighed over the story instead of salivating over the seven-bedroom mansion with a view and a pool and sauna and fifty acres of forestland.

Maybe it was a weird litmus test, but Beau could tell a lot about a woman through her reaction to Turtledove Place.

I'm not testing her. Okay, maybe he was. But of course, he'd already seen her reaction. *She loves the house for the love it represents, not for the property value or the view or the social status.*

44

Could she be for real? Maybe she was a great actress. Her sister had sure fooled Beau at first, too.

Sophie's not Tracey. But they did look so similar, it was hard to keep that straight sometimes. Which wasn't fair to Sophie, but still.

After the snow fight, the kids were wiped out. Sophie put them down in their rooms with a stack of storybooks that hadn't been cracked in months. "For every two books you read, you get to decorate a cookie tonight."

"I'm going to read all of them!" Adele grabbed a huge pile.

"No, me! Leave me some," Mac whined.

Sophie straightened it out, and then shut the door with the words, "Quiet time, guys. One hour."

An hour! Of quiet time? Unheard of at Turtledove Place lately. "Impressive negotiation skills," he said. "How are you going to spend your hour?"

"Did you say you wanted to show me the grounds of the property?" She headed down the staircase. "I'm sorry I haven't made time to appreciate them. I know you love them, and it's important to you."

Beau gripped the handrail. "I'd love to give you a sunset tour."

With layers of hoodies intact, they braved the whipping wind, snow crystals peppering his cheeks as he led her trouncing up the path and through the new snowfall toward the woods.

Would she like the view from Mom's special overlook?

"It's breathtaking. Tonight the sunset is just spectacular." Sophie relaxed against Mom's bench, gazing out at the lake, rather than at the seven-bedroom mansion, like the greedy women had who'd come before her. "And to think, you can watch its colors change any evening you want out here. I bet this place was special to someone."

"Yeah. Mom came here a lot with a lawn chair to watch just this scene unfold." Beau settled down beside her. Too bad he hadn't thought of bringing a thermos up here to share a hot beverage. "Finally, Pops installed this seat just for her. She came most nights. She called it her ponder place."

Sophie turned from the sunset and faced him. "Tell me about your mom and stepdad."

"What about them?" Sweet that she'd ask, but that was Sophie. Or so he was learning.

"How did they ... happen?"

That was a good way to put it. A couple in love *happened*. "My mom met Pops late in life."

"After you were already married."

"Yeah." To Tracey. Bad move. He cleared his throat to clear that memory. "I think they caught each other off-guard. He'd been unhappily married to someone who didn't appreciate Tazewell Solutions. Mom had been married to my dad."

"He'd been in the military, right?" Sophie looked out at the pink sky. "But if I remember correctly, you weren't close to him."

How could she remember that? "I joined up to see whether I could understand him better. At first I wanted to be a helicopter pilot like he was. Fly the Huey, but I ended up with other assignments."

"Did he die in battle?"

Not even close. "He never saw battle. Instead, he saw the bottom of every bottle he ever met." Which was why Beau's parents had divorced when he was younger and why Beau hadn't ever and wouldn't ever touch the stuff, one of several points of contention between him and Tracey. "It turned out I loved the Air Force, even though it didn't help me understand him."

"It probably did more than you think."

No. Not yet, anyway.

"Do you miss it? I heard you made captain before leaving active duty."

He did miss it, but not enough to leave Tazewell Solutions. He needed to make Pops proud of him—and the best way was to convince the military to give them the contract for the software their engineers had spent the past six years developing.

"Yes and no. I like that the kids and I can be in one place, and not move around all the time, like we would if I were on active duty."

"And what a perfect place to raise them." Sophie looked out over the view. "It's really beautiful here. The forest, the lake, the sky. How precious that my niece and nephew can grow up somewhere like Turtledove Place."

46

Yeah, now that she mentioned it. "I guess it's the silver lining." Of all the dark clouds that had marred the year. "Thanks."

"For what?"

"For showing me the view."

***

Back inside, Sophie read a text. Beau didn't intend to look, but her phone screen was practically aimed at him. It said something about registration for her boards, an online study group, and a fee coming due.

Guilt, guilt, guilt. He was detaining her from her life.

"Okay, kids, Aunt Sophie is going to study. You two go outside." He bundled the kids and got his own coat to take them to play a game. "You do have something you can study, don't you? Even with the internet down?"

She nodded sheepishly. "I brought one textbook."

"Good. Do it." If he kept her happy while she was here, maybe she'd be willing to show up more often. It would be so much easier with her help. It was already, just today, easier to be dad to the kids.

"We're going to play a game called *shovel the driveway*." He led them outside. "Who wants the red shovel and who wants blue?"

An hour later, they were only halfway finished, and both kids were flagging.

"Can we stop now?"

They couldn't go back inside yet, or they'd disturb her.

"What would Aunt Sophie do to make this fun?" Beau asked.

Adele leaned against her shovel. "She'd make it into a game."

Wouldn't she, though. Beau clapped his mittens together. "Let's have a contest." He lined them up like two race cars at a starting line, fired off an imaginary gun, and sent them to the end of the driveway, shovels down. It worked. Adele won the trip up to the road, and Mac won the return race. *Good for Adele.*

He switched shovels on them. "I think Adele might have had an advantage because she had the red shovel and it's naturally faster." Mac used the red for the next pass and won.

The game was working. Soon, progress was evident and the end was in

47

sight, and the driveway was clear enough to at least be able to pull out.

"That was fun, Dad." Adele hugged her shovel. "You're almost as fun as Aunt Sophie."

Triumph achieved.

"Yeah"—Mac chomped a mouthful of snow from his mitten—"good job, Dad."

A compliment. From a kid. Wow. "Maybe I should ask more often what Aunt Sophie would do." Beau gathered their snow shovels.

"What would I do?" Sophie, carrying another shovel, walked out through the snow in a fitted white parka that hugged her waist and hips. Did she really have a figure like that? Nah, it had to be the coat. Or the cold making him see things that weren't there.

"Wow," she said. "You guys worked fast. It's already finished. I wanted to help."

"Aw," Mac whined. "You missed it. And it was fun. I beat Adele twice." Then he brightened. "We could do Mrs. Chan's driveway next door."

Uh, seriously? Beau was a little beat, and the kids were, too. But a look from Sophie taught him he'd better not squelch a generous thought in a child. "Great idea, Mac," he said. "That's the Christmas spirit."

They tromped through the snow to the house next door. Mrs. Chan's driveway equaled Turtledove Place's, but the game expedited the work. Sophie even put a new twist on it, making a race between adults versus kids. Her ice-blue eyes sparkled like the crystals on the surface of the snow.

And the way that parka fit. Interesting. There are some heretofore unnoticed curves on Sophie.

During the so-called game, the kids were a little way down the driveway. Sophie turned to him.

"How did you end up at Tazewell Solutions instead of on active duty?"

Beau explained Pops and the reasoning—that Beau had the military background, and that he was the son Pops never had. "How could I refuse?"

"So you switched to the Reserve to keep serving?" She looked up at him. "Thank you for your service."

It was a phrase he heard a lot around Sugarplum Falls, but it seemed different coming from Sophie. Like it wasn't a rote repetition. Like she really meant it.

"You're working a job at Darlington Speech Clinic, you said?"

She described her internship a little. "I love working with the kids. They're the best part of it all. I can't wait until I have my certificate and get to do it full time."

Good thing he'd let her get some studying in today, or he'd have been wallowing in guilt right about now. "You're great with kids."

She smiled up at him, showing all her teeth, and her pale blue eyes were merry. "How do you know?"

"I've seen you with mine."

"Aw, well. I can't help loving Adele and Mac. They belong to me."

Beau paused. Yeah, in a way, they did.

He asked after her parents. He'd been more or less out of touch with them for a while, except when he'd called Mrs. Hawkins for advice on taking care of the kids.

What he didn't ask Sophie was about her personal life. She had to be dating someone. She didn't seem remotely desperate or scheming like those other women Beau kept running across. Everything about Sophie was a reservoir of calm.

Mrs. Chan came out with caramel apples, each with a label from Sugarbabies Bake Shop. "You children are wonderful." She handed one to Adele, and then one to Mac, focusing on the kids with her compliments. They soaked up the praise—and the apples, beaming and a little sweaty around their hairlines. Shoveling was a good workout.

"We just got hit by the Christmas spirit is all." Mac took a huge bite, and Adele nodded, providing emphasis.

Mrs. Chan winked at Beau. "I must say, your wife is even prettier than I remember, Beau. I might not get out as much as I used to, but I'm so glad the two of you have moved your family next door to me. It's wonderful to have a young family in the neighborhood. Brings it such life."

"Oh, we're not—" Sophie got interrupted.

"And your children!" Mrs. Chan gushed. "They are so well-behaved and polite. You two are venturing into Perfect Parent territory." She snickered, gave them Christmas-gloved waves, and went back inside.

With apples on sticks in hand, they hiked back next door, but the kids ran ahead.

As soon as only Sophie could hear him, Beau cringed and said, "That was awkward."

"Nah." Sophie sighed. "She's just being kind. Genuine kindness can't be taken as awkward."

Maybe. Of course, Sophie might not have minded being told she was prettier than Tracey. Was Mrs. Chan right about that? Maybe Beau should look sometime. "Well, I therefore decree we shall fraudulently reside in *perfect parent territory* in silence."

"It's for the best," she said gravely, placing a silencing finger to her full, pink lips. Her pale skin glowed pink just at the apples of her cheeks.

Huh. When she'd been shoveling snow, she definitely had a pretty glow. One that tickled the back of his spine until he looked away. She was his ex-wife's *sister*.

They followed the kids' footprints through the vast front acreage of Turtledove Place, walking in and out of the cold, dappled shade made by the trees that lined its drive.

"While I was studying, the internet started working again, and I checked the weather report."

"Oh?" Maybe a storm could dump fifteen feet of snow on Sugarplum Falls and cut off all travel so she'd be snowed in until spring. Or at least until after he'd finished the Department of Defense contract submission.

"The second storm is going to change direction and not hit Sugarplum Falls. The pass will likely be open in the morning."

They reached the porch and stood on its dry slats a moment. "Huh. Good." A different word than *good* came to mind. It rhymed with *hammit*.

"But now that I've studied all I can stand to for the day, I'd love to entertain the kids while you get some work done."

Normally, the kids kept noise at deafening levels, and such a plan was a joke. "You know, I might actually get something done from home today." He

50

meant it, and not just due to the promise of quiet. Something creaked and groaned inside Beau, like the sound of Sugar Lake in the spring when the weather warmed up. It wasn't the deafening crack of the actual thaw—not yet—but there were signs of one.

He might even be able to think his way out of the mental blockade preventing him from completing the government contract application.

Of course, it could be a coincidence, Sophie being here at this moment. They said the passage of time healed all wounds. Maybe Sophie had shown up at Turtledove Place at the exact moment that his healing from Tracey's betrayal finally kicked in.

Yeah. And reindeer can fly.

***

The next morning, the roads were open by dawn. Sophie packed her bag and headed downstairs. Beau toted her bag for her. Why had that storm veered? Why did she have to leave? What was he going to do in—ugh—seven hours when school let out?

Beau was adrift. Bereft. Flat-out bummed.

Can't you stay? The words perched on his lips.

Adele and Mac appeared at the banister along the loft area. "Aunt Sophie. You're going?" Adele's voice trembled. "Just when we were starting to love you here?"

Exactly. Well, loving *having* you here, Beau would have phrased it.

"Yeah," Mac said, followed by three loud sneezes: *Atchoo! Atchoo! Atchoo!* "I bill biss youb." His nose and eyes were red enough it was visible from down here.

Sophie turned to Beau. Their gazes met.

"He's sick," she whispered.

Beau's stomach filled with lead. Miss work at Tazewell again today? With the deadline looming and only one evening of progress on his contract application? Yesterday he'd pushed through a few sections, but he was nowhere near completion.

She looked torn, her gaze darting back and forth between Mac and Beau, as if she didn't know what to do. Love for Mac was there, and some kind of pity for Beau.

Beau couldn't bear pity. Not from Sophie. "Go on. You have work today."

"I'm an intern. They don't *need* me. They don't even pay me."

She wasn't being paid? "But they're expecting you, right?"

Sophie lowered her voice. "Tell me the honest truth, Beau. You have something massive going on at Tazewell Solutions." She put her hands on her hips as if she wouldn't budge until he answered honestly. "You're not saying, but I take it a great deal is riding on whatever is on your plate right now."

He closed his eyes, not willing to divulge everything, but his head gave a tiny, involuntary nod.

"That settles it." She turned to the kids, speaking at full volume again. "Mac, you're staying home. Adele, you're getting ready to catch the school bus." She turned back to him. "Beau, you're going to work."

"You—you're staying?" Beau stuttered.

"You're staying?" Adele shrieked. "Just because Mac got sick? If I feel sick too, would you stay even longer?"

The kids skipped back toward their bedrooms.

Sophie turned to Beau. "Maybe it's presumptuous of me to announce it without consulting you, but I'm staying—either until Mac is better or until Christmas. Whichever comes first."

"Sophie." There were no words to express the relief. "I—"

She interrupted, breaking into a rambling speech. "Or, until you find a new nanny. Not sure. Until whenever it feels right to go—which, yeah. It doesn't today." She folded her arms and planted her feet. "I don't know exactly what's going on at Tazewell and what you're not saying, but whatever it is, I simply cannot see how you're going to manage everything on your plate without serious, full-time help. So, I'm staying." She unfolded her arms from across her chest.

Then, her gaze softened, and a sheepish little smile tugged at one side of her mouth. "I mean, if it's all right with you."

Chapter 7

Sophie

Holy frijoles. Talk about the bravest discourse Sophie had ever made in her life.

Beau obviously had more than he could handle alone right now, and no one to help him. Worse, the kids had no one.

As the younger sister of the culprit who'd put Beau in this predicament, it fell to Sophie to correct it.

"I'm staying. If it's all right with you."

Beau didn't answer. He just stared at her—an indecipherable look on his face. Was this the moment when he admitted to her why he'd banned her from his house all those years ago? Would he now tell her to get along, little dogie, she wasn't wanted at Turtledove Place?

Her insecurities didn't gel with what he'd said earlier about wanting her help with creating Christmas. But that was before she announced she was forcing herself on his family full time.

She bit her lower lip, awaiting his verbal response. She searched his hazel eyes for an answer, and only saw relief there. *Please let that be relief.*

"Sophie, I—" he said, when Sophie's phone rang.

Dr. Vaughn. "Uh, sorry. It's my boss." Er, my boyfriend. "Think about what I said, but don't tell me to go home. I won't. Not with Mac sick."

Beau gave a dry laugh behind her when she turned aside to answer the still-ringing phone.

"Hey, Dr. Vaughn."

"When are you going to start calling me Matt?" Sophie could picture him adjusting his dark-rimmed glasses.

"I figure you're already in the office for the day, so Dr. Vaughn makes sense." She stepped from the mud room into the kitchen. "I guess you noticed I'm not there yet today."

"Or yesterday. I heard about the avalanche. Just checking to see if you're all right. Do I need to rent a snow plow and come rescue you from Sugarplum Snowdrift? I did some calculations, and with the right size of snowplow, I could move approximately eighteen cubic feet of snow per hour, which means, depending on the size of the avalanche, I could have you out of Sugarplum Falls and back at the clinic within, oh, three days. If I work nonstop."

That was sweet. "I'm all right. But …" How should she tell him what she'd just hurled at Beau? Especially since Beau hadn't responded in the affirmative yet, and might not. "I'm not going to make it today. Or tomorrow either. In fact, I might have to stay away until the end of the year."

"Remember, I just did the math for you." Matt chortled. "I mean, this isn't the era of *Seven Brides for Seven Brothers* where you'll be stuck in the mountains until spring with a stranger who you end up marrying." He laughed, but his joke hit Sophie's ear like a bell with a hand against it to stop its ringing. "Sophie?"

"Don't worry. It's my brother-in-law. He sees me as a kid-sister, not a snowbound captive future wife." Barbs scraped her throat with the words. "It is a situation, though, that my sister caused, and he needs help. His nannies have all been"—what was accurate without being too offensive?—"skanks."

"Oooh. Skanks. No one wants their kids babysat by skanks."

"Or their niece and nephew."

"I see." Matt sounded like he sort of did see. "Family comes first." Resignation filled his tone. "But Lachlan Llewellyn has an appointment again Friday, and his mom called to request you specifically."

Cute Lachlan. "I wish I could be there. He needs help with his *R*s next."

The conversation stalled. Finally, Matt said, "What about Christmas, Sophie?"

What about it? Her parents would still be on their anniversary cruise, so that would be different. It'd be sad not to spend the big day with Mac and Adele, but Beau wouldn't really want her intruding on his family time—even if Mrs. Chan next door had asserted they were a good-looking couple, they were not, in fact, a couple.

"What about it?" she repeated, this time aloud.

"I was hoping you could spend it with me. Maybe … meet my parents."

Meet his parents! Oh. Ohhhh. "Matt, I—" But they weren't even dating exclusively. Some days Sophie wasn't even sure she and Matt were dating at all. It was dinners on Friday nights, and a little friendly banter at the office. But was it *meet the parents* level for him?

"Don't decide now," he jumped in, as if patting out the flames of a sudden haystack fire. "Just call me now and then. I'll be missing you."

Missing her. Never since she'd started seeing him, more or less accidentally over the summer, had Matt sounded sentimental.

"Tell Lachlan Llewellyn hello, and to practice his *L*s for me, would you?" And then she added, "I'll miss you, too, Matt." She hung up and turned to see Beau standing in the doorway beneath the turtledove transom.

"I didn't mean to eavesdrop." Guilt strolled across his posture. "Was that your office? Tell me you're not going to be fired if you miss work for the month."

She shook her head. How much had he overheard? Did Beau know she was dating her boss? What would he even think of her about that? Maybe nothing, but she wasn't sure what she thought of herself. Now her face was blazing, probably the color of Rudolph's nose.

"They don't fire interns."

"Okay, that's good."

It was? "So you're okay if I stay?"

"Okay! I'm ecstatic. Grateful. Floored that you'd do it."

Whew! She exhaled too loudly and shifted into high gear rambling. "While I'm here, I'll help Adele study for that spelling bee she's obsessed with. And if it's okay with you, I'd like to help Mac with his speech."

"You will?"

"Just to keep my skills up. But only if you agree."

"I more than agree."

Excellent! Adrenaline kicked in. "I have lots of plans for making a good Christmas. How about one activity as a family per day, if you can spare the time? Nothing too long. Twenty minutes, tops, since you're super busy. You focus on your work, but since I'm organizing the fun, you can still give the kids a good holiday season. It'll be simple stuff, like a board game, or making dinner together, a quick snow race."

She was fire-hosing him with plans and probably sounded bossy or wild-brained, but he didn't look irritated. Instead, he stepped toward her and placed his arms around her in the world's most awkward hug, part two.

"You are really something." He patted her back, and it took all her will not to relax into his arms. "Can I add some plans, too?"

He certainly could.

***

That evening, Beau texted to say he'd be home late. Too late to make dinner with them, which had been her first Christmas tradition idea. But the text was so considerate and apologetic, she could hardly hold it against him.

He's texting me. Sophie stared at the letters on the screen of her phone. Her first ever text from Beau. Maybe the last. She'd never delete it.

Instead, Sophie recreated the Calzones-with-Aunt-Sophie tradition, this time at their own house instead of hers.

Just as the pans came out of the oven, Beau walked in the door. He looked tired, but not haggard. And he mouthed an apology.

She waved it off, but she kept staring at his mouth for a second, until Adele hollered.

"Daddy, look! We made you a pizza pocket!" Adele waved the plate with his pepperoni calzone at him. "I told Aunt Sophie you like green olives, not black."

Beau rubbed Adele's head and then turned to Sophie and mouthed *I'm sorry* again.

She shrugged it off. "We had a great time. Now, let's eat."

He joined them at the table, leading them in grace. "We thank thee, Lord, for this bounty and for Aunt Sophie."

Both the kids shouted their amens. Maybe she should work on reverence with them a little.

"I have a family Christmas activity planned for us tonight." Beau took a bite of his calzone, and then his eye met Sophie's. "Wow." He spoke through his large bite. "You guys made this? It's really good."

Over dinner, the kids talked about their day. Mac's cold was eighty percent better. He'd be able to go to school again soon. Maybe even tomorrow. Then Adele asked Beau to finish his announcement. "What is the activity, Daddy? Are we going to cut down a Christmas tree?"

"No, Adele. Not tonight," Sophie jumped to say. "It's probably something short. Your dad has some work to finish for his company."

He gave her a grateful-looking nod. "No, but let's do it soon because that's a good idea, Adele."

Adele beamed. It was sweet, and it seemed like she'd been starving for it.

Sophie put her elbow on the table and almost sighed and rested her chin on her hand. Beau always made Sophie's heart flutter, but when he was being a great dad, her blood turned into rivers of lava. She drank three huge gulps of ice water, which helped. A little. But Beau was still in the room, and Sophie was still hyper-aware of his every breath.

After dinner and cleanup, Beau sent them all to the living room.

"You ready for my plan? It's a game," Beau announced. "Should I light a fire in the fireplace before we start?"

"No!" Sophie shouted. The room fell silent, and all eyes were on her. "I mean, heh-heh. It's already warm in here." *If you count me as the molten lump of aching desire.* "Let's get started so you can finish up some work, right?"

It ended up Beau's idea was a Christmas charades card game, which turned out to be hilarious. It took about five rounds before Mac finally got the concept of not saying anything during his pantomimes, but he finally caught on.

"I get the last turn," Beau said. He drew a card from the stack and stood in front of the empty hearth, while everyone else sat on the sofa to guess. "Here goes." He waved his hand like a choral conductor.

"It's a song!" Adele shouted, guessing right. "Silent Night!"

He shook his head. Then he made kissy lips.

"Ew!" Mac shouted. "Gross!"

Sophie burst out laughing.

"Daddy," Adele scolded. "No."

Beau broke the rules, saying aloud, "You still haven't guessed my clues."

Next he mimed pinching fingers above his head. Next, he made that universal sign for the figure of Marilyn Monroe, the hourglass figure. Next, he patted his belly and made a sweeping rounded motion over the top of it, like a belly, and bouncing it three times while mouthing *ho, ho, ho.*

Oh, Sophie knew this one. It was that song about the kid who woke up in the night and saw her parents making out near the Christmas tree. Not a favorite, necessarily. What was it called?

Beau repeated his four moves—the mistletoe, the kiss, the hourglass, and the belly. The kids started shouting random things.

"Love song at Christmas?" Sophie made a stab in the dark.

"Fat person kisses pretty person?" Mac offered.

"Daddy kisses Aunt Sophie and then she has a baby?" Adele said.

Everything stopped. Dead silent. All eyes turned to Adele.

Unfazed, she shrugged. "What? That's how Aunt Sophie looks." She mimed the hourglass. "And Daddy always looks at her like he wants to kiss her and give her a baby. Why are you all looking at me like that?"

Sophie shot to her feet. "Time for bed."

"Yeah," Mac said. "I hated that game." He grumped up the stairs. "I don't think Daddy should kiss Sophie and give her a baby unless he marries her first. That's what happened in the Bible story. They had to get married before the baby was born. I listened in church."

Oh, dear.

Oh, dear, oh, dear, oh, dear. Sophie rushed them upstairs. "Who wants a bath first? And who wants a storybook?"

Baths and stories occupied the rest of the evening, and Sophie didn't return to the fireside hearth that night. It was a blooming good thing Beau wanted nothing to do with kissing Sophie beneath the mistletoe when he played Santa Claus—since she was not their mommy. Or the mommy of any of Beau's babies. Ever.

Although I could be convinced to be so in less than a heartbeat, unfortunately.

She curled under her covers, squeezing her eyes shut to scrub away the image of Beau's kissy lips. Even in cheesy farce, they still looked impossibly kissable.

She shouldn't have stayed here. This was a mistake.

Christmas. She could make it until Christmas—physically.

Emotionally? That was still up in the air.

Chapter 8

Beau

In his office at Tazewell Solutions, Beau stared at his screen, the wording of his proposal tripping him up. Again. *Airborne radar software for detecting activity through or beneath foliage canopy and in forested areas.* But it was convoluted, and who could understand it? Beau had to make it clearer, or they'd never get the contract. He pushed back his office chair and paced the room.

Beau flopped down and rocked in his office chair. He couldn't concentrate at work this afternoon. At all. Why? One answer: Adele's shout the other night that Sophie was the curvaceous figure he'd drawn, and encouraging him to kiss her and—ahem—give her a baby. Gulp. The memory invaded his thoughts like one of those earworm Christmas pop songs about hippopotamuses, rolling on an unstoppable loop.

He reached over to the shelf and spun the propeller on the model of the C-124 cargo plane to think about principles of aerodynamics. Weight, lift, thrust, drag. Bernoulli's Lift, for one. Speed plus airflow created lift.

None of that helped. Sophie's figure in that white parka the other day kept popping into his brain. It was strange. Yeah, she was pretty—like Mrs. Chan had said—in a fresh, untouched way. And though she and Tracey could pass for each other in a juvenile switch-prank, she didn't have any of the steam coming off her that Tracey had exuded. *At least until she switched off the steam valves toward him.* Sophie didn't seem to *want* to put off steam toward him.

Besides, she'd told someone on the phone she'd been missing him. Boyfriend back in Darlington? Boss? One and the same? Obviously, she had another man in her life.

If so, then why was Sophie popping into his mind at the worst times all day? Maybe he had one of those complexes, where the rescued fell for the savior. Because she really was saving him.

Who is the guy she's dating? No, no. He didn't care. He couldn't. He wouldn't, except that if she missed someone, she might be inclined to leave. And if she left, then ... *I'm alone again in the fight.*

Beau put his head in his hands. It was heavier than usual.

"Hey, there," a soft but rich feminine voice said.

Beau lifted his head.

Olympia Barron leaned against the doorway of his office. "You look like you're far away." She undulated into the room and sank seductively into the chair across from his desk. Okay, maybe it wasn't purposely sexy in a midday office visit, but every time Olympia moved, she emanated seduction. "What can I do to bring you back and help you finish our application?"

Oh, so that's what this was about. Not actually checking on his well-being but the well-being of their application. That was fair. Professional. *Different from the Gemmas of the world, at least.*

"I'm getting there. I've made some progress." Not much, but a little. Each night this week after family time, Sophie had swooped in and taken care of the kids so that he could work from home in the evenings undisturbed. And Sophie had done other things, as well, like making sure he ate breakfast before he left each morning, and creating a family dinner at night. She was bringing order to the chaos. "According to the little green completion bar on the screen, I'm fifteen percent done."

"Beau." Olympia's voice was sultry. "We need to submit it."

"And we will." He scrubbed a hand through the short spikes of his military haircut. "I've got one section not coming together, but once it does, the rest will go smoothly."

"Anything I can do to ... you know. *Unblock you?*"

Why did that sound so dirty? Probably because Beau had had baby-making on his subconscious mind ever since the charades game.

"This contract is as important to me as it is to you. This *company* is as important to me as it is to you." Her lips were full and candy-apple red—and they spoke the truth: Beau and Olympia held an equal number of shares in the corporation, and they both stood to lose everything if this contract didn't succeed. *Or if it didn't get submitted at all.* As it was, Tazewell's coffers were running on fumes, and he might need to borrow money for a cash infusion to make payroll right before Christmas.

Pressure much?

"Thanks, but I've got it."

"All right. Just checking." Olympia stood to go. "I'm here for you, Beau. Anything you need." She looked over her shoulder and paused at the door with one, long-nailed hand on the doorframe like a caress. "Anything."

Oooh.

And she was gone.

Beau swatted against the image of her hip-sway and turned his eyes back to his screen. His step-aunt's advice, however, chose this moment to resurface in his brain.

You need a wife. Olympia Barron is single and attractive.

Air seethed through Beau's teeth. Attractive, yes. No question. A man would have to be blind not to—

If you showed the least hint of interest ...

It wasn't the worst idea. The kids did need stability. They thrived in a steady, structured home, as he was seeing daily for the past week. Olympia was as structured as they came, at least at work. Very organized, almost to a fault. No way would Mac and Adele lack for oversight and order if Olympia were at Beau's side parenting them.

It was something to think about. Later. After he finished this blasted application.

He turned back to his computer where the letters and fillable form boxes swam on the screen. It was no good. He was getting nowhere this afternoon. And dang it, his shoulder was collecting all the stress again, in a fierce, throbbing knot of pain near his neck.

He rolled his head and neck to work it out. Useless.

Well, even if not the application, Beau might as well be accomplishing *something*. Anything. The only other goal he had right now was to give Mac and Adele a good Christmas. He packed up his briefcase and checked the noontime text from Sophie again.

Depending on your schedule, if you come home early, we have something fun we can do. No pressure. I'll do it with the kids if you can't

make it.

She didn't say what it was, probably so as not to make him feel guilty if he missed out. But whatever it was, even shoveling Mrs. Chan's driveway again, it had to be better than spinning his wheels and gnashing his teeth in frustration here.

He grabbed his coat and headed for the door.

He was going home.

Chapter 9

Sophie

"I don't know, kids. Your dad may or may not make it tonight." She finished putting the rice and pork chops on plates and set them on the table. "He's really busy right now." Doing what, he hadn't shared, but it was obviously important. Bless him for making time every night for something festive, like that Candy Kingdom board game, or taking a plate of cookies to Mrs. Chan, even though he'd refused to join their song when they broke into "We Wish You a Merry Christmas." Buzzkill much? It was weird, since he really did have a great voice, last time Sophie had heard him use it to sing. "If he can't come, we'll go another time."

"Go where?" In walked Beau, pulling off his scarf and coat and striding toward the table and making Sophie's heart do a little flip. "I heard you guys have fun plans. But I have an idea, too."

"No, Daddy! I don't want any more charades," Mac whined. The kid had a whine on him. Sophie would have to try to train it out of him as a Christmas gift to herself. "I want to see the lights."

"Lights?" Beau sat down at his place at the table. "Wow, this looks good." He leaned over his pork chop and inhaled. "Smells amazing. What lights? I was thinking of roasting marshmallows in front of the fire in our very own fireplace."

Uh, fireplace? With Beau in its glow? No. Nopey-nope-nope. Because it wouldn't be out by the time the kids went to bed, and then it would just be Sophie and Beau in front of a warm, inviting, will-melting flame.

Sophie's self-control could not be trusted in front of a fireplace. She had five bad-choice, Mr. Wrong makeouts during college to prove it. Yikes.

"I want marshmallows!" Mac shouted. "I love marshmallows!" More shouting.

"I wanted to see the lights on the falls," Adele moaned. "I heard from Daisy at school that they're really pretty, prettier than a unicorn's mane." She shoved her elbow on the table and plopped her chin onto her hand, propping her dejected head there. "Can't we?"

Beau nodded. "Unicorn's mane, eh?" He met Sophie's eyes, and amusement danced there. For a second, she was his co-conspirator, and they were sharing a joke between adults. Maybe Sophie wasn't just a kid to him.

"Prettier than all the Pegasus wings put together. Daisy knows, too. She has five of the Pegasus pony dolls with the rainbow wings."

"I like Pegasus wings," Sophie said. "How about you, Mac?" She turned to the kid. "Do you think flying horses are cool? Like the ones in that video game, *Horsefly*?"

"I like horse wings," Mac said. "Will the lights be like that? Can we see those?"

"I guess we'll see." She shrugged, turning to Beau, trying to hide her relief. "We'll do the fire another time, maybe?"

"Sure." Beau nodded. "But let's not wait too long. There are some fireside discussions I'd like to have with you"—he lowered his voice—"after the kids go to bed."

Rrrrch! Needle-scratch across the vinyl record of her heart. "Um, okay?" she squeaked. "Let's plan that sometime." Later. After her self-control had been bolstered with galvanized steel.

After dinner, the kids went to wash up and change into pajamas so they could watch the show from the car, which was how things were done. Good thinking, Sugarplum Falls activities organizers, considering that subzero weather wasn't great for outdoor activities at night.

While Sophie washed dishes, Beau dried them.

"I saw what you did back there." He took a drinking glass straight from her hand, brushing her wet fingers and nearly making her drop the fragile item. "Peace brokering on a high level. You could list that on your résumé."

"Thanks for not being mad that I led them another direction."

"I still want a fire with you."

"With me? Don't you mean marshmallows with the kids?"

"Sure, but also with you. To plan out the traditions I want to set with the kids. I need to consult."

"Can't we consult here?" With our hands in dishwater? Where it was safe?

"I think best with a fire."

How ironic. She thought worst with a fire.

Beau rubbed the side of his neck. "I think staring at the flames soothes my subconscious, helps me let go of my nerves. Then my creativity can go wild."

Sophie froze. At twenty-five, she was far too young for cardiac arrest, but in this moment, she totally qualified as a candidate with Beau's mention of going wild and letting go of his nerves.

Sweet marmalade, that was not something she should let lodge in her mind, swirling, tempting her, drawing her into its enticing imagery …

She dropped a drinking glass. It landed in the sink, not breaking, but it probably should have. *He loses his inhibitions? Did he just say that to me?* She willed herself to keep her breathing rate steady. No. He'd said fires soothe his nerves. *Sophie* was the one who lost inhibitions. *Keep it straight.*

Nevertheless, a little movie played a ridiculous scenario in her mind's eye: *Sophie with her legs curled on the couch, her head resting on Beau's chest, his fingers twirling the ends of a lock of her hair, dragging the tips of it across the cupid's bow of his lips and humming sweet nothings at her.*

She dropped *another* glass.

Crack! This one did break in the sink.

"Oops. Sorry. I'll clean that up." Yeah, she'd better ix-nay all thoughts of that type right now. He'd fired a nanny for throwing herself at him. Not that Sophie could blame the girl—Beau was a worthy target for throwing. But still. He had standards, and they didn't include interfering with younger women who were in his beautiful home to help out with his children.

"I'll do a solo brainstorm, and then maybe we can talk ideas over. For traditions." Not for how to let themselves go creatively wild. "The Waterfall Lights at the frozen waterfall tonight are a good start, and"—she scrambled for an idea—"there's that hot chocolate event this weekend."

"Oh, the festival. Yeah. I'd like to take you to that."

Her? "The kids and me, you mean."

"Yeah, of course."

Of course. Okay, her imagination officially ran rampant. It was stupid. She had to redeem her brain and her composure, fast. "What ideas did *you* have in mind for yearly Christmas activities? For your children and you?"

Beau thought a minute and then said, "It's not a big deal, but a Christmas swim would be good."

"You'd better not be talking about one of those polar bear plunge things in the frozen water of Sugar Lake, because I am not your girl for that." Who was she kidding? She was his girl for anything he asked.

"No, just in the pool downstairs."

"There's a pool downstairs?"

"You mean you haven't seen it? I swim laps every morning."

"The house doesn't smell like chlorine."

"That's because it's natural spring-fed. Constantly running water means no chlorine required."

Mountain springs! "This spring-fed pool. Is it, um, heated?" Cold water was a serious fear of hers. Military macho man that he was, Beau could probably take a morning swim in an unheated pool in the Sugarplum Falls climate, but Sophie? No way. Irrational as it may have been, she'd always suffered from nightmares about freezing to death in icy waters, falling through a hole in a frozen lake while skating and not being able to find the hole to exit, drowning and freezing at once, without a friendly St. Bernard to pull her to safety and warmth.

Before he could answer, Adele came barreling down the stairs.

"It's already past seven o'clock. The Waterfall Lights show is starting really soon. Can't we go? Now?"

Beau turned to Sophie. "I never should have taught her to tell time."

They piled into Beau's SUV. Sophie sat at Beau's side, and the kids were in the back seat. *Don't get used to this. Don't. It's not where you'll belong long term.* Maybe not, but it felt pretty natural just then.

They pulled into a jammed parking lot of the overlook at Sugarplum Falls. Beau kept the engine and the heater running—bless him.

"It's so beautiful." Sophie gasped as Christmas lights danced against the ice in spectacular, colorful patterns. Beau tuned the radio to a short-distance station that played music that was perfectly timed to the lights' patterns. The effect was a light show even better than a rainbow unicorn's wings.

"This is so cool!" Mac was loving it. He came up and sat in Sophie's lap. "Look, it's Santa! Is that the real Santa?"

Different holiday scenes projected in colored lights onto the tower of frozen waterfall, changing to the beats of the music on the radio—everything from Santa in a sleigh to a nativity scene complete with sheep and donkeys and shepherds at the manger.

Adele perched on the console between the driver and passenger seats. They smooshed together like a happy little family.

Someone knocked on the window. "Hot cocoa? Warm cider?" A kid with a name tag reading *Declan* held four-pack drink holders up for offer. "They're from The Cider Press, so I can guarantee their deliciousness. Family discount."

Beau bought one for each of them, plus an apple cider doughnut also on offer from the bakery at the Sugarplum Falls Art Museum's cafeteria. "They make incredible doughnuts."

Mmm. So they did. Sophie bit into the soft, yeasty, cakey deliciousness. Fruit and spice and sweetness did a dance on her tongue to the rhythm of the music and lights all around.

Declan bowed, took his cash—and his tip—and thanked them. "Merry Christmas. Bye!" He ran to the next car.

Cute kid. If he was the essence of the young people of Sugarplum Falls, this was definitely a good place to raise kids.

The lights were ingenious, keeping time with the music piping into the cabin of their cozy SUV. After an hour, the show restarted to play familiar patterns, and some cars beside them peeled away. Sophie looked down. Mac was asleep in her lap. Adele yawned.

"I didn't see a unicorn," she said. "Can we watch a Christmas rainbow unicorn movie to make up for it?"

Um, no? "We'll see."

Sophie put Mac into his seatbelt, and Adele buckled herself in. They headed back to Turtledove Place. Beau had been oddly quiet.

Once the kids were settled in their beds, he stopped Sophie in the hallway outside their rooms. Wall sconces lit the air between them, creating a romantic glow. Sophie loitered instead of going off to bed, having a hard time keeping her eyes off Beau's gaze, which seemed to be lingering on her eyes.

"So, Sophie. I hope that thing didn't bother you the other day."

About the fact he wouldn't sing when they went caroling? "I did wish you'd joined us when we sang." Beau had a great voice. He even used to play the guitar, back when he and Tracey had been dating. It was crazy that he held out on his kids that way. What kind of example did he think he was setting?

He looked at her flatly. "Oh, caroling? Yeah. Sorry. I don't sing."

"You should sing. Not singing is like refusing to let happiness into your life. Especially at Christmastime."

Beau blinked a couple of times and said, "Noted. What I meant was the charades game of awkwardness. How that ended up. I hope *that* didn't bother you too much."

Oh, that. Suddenly the air was charged between them in a different way entirely. "Um …" What was she supposed to say? That she loved everything about the idea? Because, yeah. Not an appropriate response.

"The song was actually 'I Saw Mommy Kissing Santa Claus.' In case you never figured it out."

"Oh." Sophie fought against the images, and the feelings they elicited. *Giving Sophie a baby,* Mac had shouted. "The pantomimes you chose—they do make sense."

"Right?" He looked relieved, leaning casually against the wall beneath the light. "So you're not mad?"

Ha. "You'll have to try harder than that to make me mad, Beau." Harder than making kiss-lips at her. "I'm a big girl. I can handle the kids' antics."

"They were definitely antics, weren't they?" He smiled broadly, smoothing every crevasse of frown lines and sinking entirely new ones for the smile. "I'm so glad someone who loves them is with me."

A little earthquake trembled at the bottom of her stomach because *oh, my goodness!* that was the smile Beau had worn back when he was nothing but an ROTC college student visiting her classroom, and making her little heart go pitter-pat by talking about planes and making her dream of a future with him. That smile. Right there in the light of this dim hallway that made his pupils large and her desire for him the biggest thing in her world.

I can't. Sophie clenched her stomach muscles to halt the tremors. "I'm your wife's sister, Beau. Of course I love them."

"My ex-wife—let's be clear. And to be clearer, I don't even think of her as my wife anymore." His smile fled. "Trust me."

Geez. Why had she brought up Tracey? Tracey was a smile-killer.

Then again, the accident confirmed Sophie's suspicions that he had no use for her useless sister. Not anymore.

"Do you want to go downstairs and brainstorm some activities? I'll build a fire like I promised."

Sophie snapped to attention, her mind grasping for a less-dangerous scenario. "How about the Hot Chocolate Festival? It's Saturday—tomorrow, that is." Anything to change the subject. "The only catch is, it'll take a lot longer than the nightly twenty minutes we've been demanding of you. More like an hour or two. I'll only get tickets if you think you can spare the time away from Tazewell."

"Get them. I'll make the time. It's important to me."

Instinctively, Sophie reached for his hand. "You're a really good dad." An electric current threatened to make its way from her fingertips to her heart. She babbled about the kids nervously for a full minute before she let go quickly, hurrying to her room before he said anything else about a fireplace.

Good night, Beau.

In her room, she checked her phone. One message waited from Vronky, and another message waited from Dr. Vaughn.

Er, Matt.

She read Vronky's text first. It had just come in the last ten minutes.

I broke up with Dorian. Oh, no! She hadn't been with him long, but he did seem like a good guy.

What happened?

He can't back up a trailer. He's a disaster at it. I'm not lowering myself to that. I know my worth.

Good for her. *Anyone else on the horizon?*

Not yet. All going well with the Cabot family? You know I really mean how are things going with Beau. Little hearts decorated his name.

All right except for one thing. I can't get past the fact when we went caroling he refused to sing. Should I let that be my can't-back-up-a-trailer deal-breaker?

There was a long pause before Vronky's reply came, but Sophie waited it out.

Think about it, Sophie. His wife left him for a singer. A greasy singer, but still. She tattooed said-singer's face on her neck.

Sophie's heart thunked. Vronky was a hundred percent correct, and Sophie had been totally wrong in pushing him into such raw, prickly territory. The fact he'd even come along on the caroling trip must have been painful enough.

She owed him an apology. Or at least the courtesy of letting him stick to his convictions until he could resolve the emotional issues surrounding music.

How insensitive of her.

Maybe looking at Matt's texts would sweep away the tide of yuckiness rising in her soul.

Are you coming home for the weekend? Surely he can watch his own kids when he's off over the weekend.

Probably true, in most cases. But instead, she texted back, *He needs me this weekend.*

If only that were true in all aspects.

She leaned against the bed's headboard and slowly pounded the back of her head against it. Matt. He had a brilliant mind, kind smile, treated her well. He was a good man. The second-best man of her acquaintance. And the first-best would never belong to Sophie.

Meanwhile, she wasn't exactly being fair to Matt. Did Matt think of Sophie and him as exclusive? He was the one bringing up meeting each other's families. *He must be more serious than I thought.* He'd given her an internship, mentored her, taken her to dinner most Fridays. Was their relationship serious-serious for him?

Jettisoning the man in her life—the one who actually wanted her, and with a track record of helping her reach all her professional goals—for someone who was utterly emotionally unavailable and who could never want her anyway would be a foolish mistake. Wouldn't it?

I don't want to hurt him. She had no idea what to do.

Chapter 10

Beau

Beau gazed down at Sophie in the dim of the hallway outside Adele and Mac's bedroom doors. She looked different in this light. Her ice-blue eyes caught a glow from somewhere. The wall sconces probably. They'd had a good night at the Waterfall Lights, and he'd been glancing at her off and on then, too. Almost involuntarily.

"Hot Chocolate Festival, huh?" he said, repeating her suggestion for tomorrow's family activity. He couldn't look away from her, even though she looked like Tracey. *Except, she didn't.* It wasn't like Sophie was some seductress like Olympia Barron in the way she walked or talked. She was just Sophie, so this undeniable attraction in the moment didn't make sense.

I don't care if it makes sense. I just want to spend a minute looking into her face. Is that wrong? He rubbed the side of his neck and shoulder where the knot was.

"But the catch is this," Sophie said, her lips gently parting as she gazed at him, making his heart speed. "It's definitely not a twenty-minute activity, so if you can't make it happen, I get it. I'll take them myself."

"That's all right. I'll make time." For some reason, he'd say yes to any suggestion of hers right now. Something had to be wrong with him. Was it the lighting? The talk of that *kissing Santa Claus* charade debacle? Whatever, it was putting Beau in a definite mood.

"Oh, good." Sophie exhaled. "For whatever reason, Adele and Mac have this idea they *need* you to be there or it won't be fun, and I'm not going to disagree with them, since it would be a lot more fun with you there, and easier to manage them in public, since, you know how they are. Please forgive me for making promises to them without checking with you first."

Oh, he forgave her all right. She wasn't leaving him high and dry. She was staying, even on the weekend, and asking him nothing more strenuous than going with her and the kids to a town Christmas party. They'd be like an intact family for once in the kids' lives this year.

Tonight's activity at the waterfall felt like that, too.

"I'll be there. No problem."

Well, it might be a problem, if Olympia discovered him there playing hooky from his computer screen. Luckily, she'd never attend something like a hot chocolate-tasting party. Sugar was her enemy, almost as much as the *enemies foreign and domestic* Tazewell Solutions promised to defend against.

"Oh, Beau." Sophie exhaled, a relieved smile spreading across her pretty mouth. "The kids will be so happy. You're a really good dad."

She reached out and brushed the side of his hand with her fingertips. A series of rolling shocks waved up his arm, and for a split second, he almost believed her words.

A good dad? Beau? Not for the past six months. Make that a year. Ever since things had gone farther and farther south with Tracey, he'd more or less checked out of his dad job. Until Sophie came.

No, Sophie was right. He needed to put in the work to make things up to the kids.

And yet, with Sophie's help, it was easy. She laid all the groundwork, and all he had to do was show up and be charming, love on the kids. Which he'd been doing all week, and it had been fun. Good times. Happiness, actually. *How does she do that?* Beau wandered down the hall to his bedroom, where he lay on top of his covers fully dressed and stared at the ceiling.

Something was going on inside him. Something was ... jarring loose.

I might actually be able to feel something again. I might be able to get married again, have an actual husband-wife relationship. A parade of faceless women floated past his mind's eye. Then, Sophie's visage appeared. Sophie! She had someone else. She was his sister-in-law. No. He brushed it aside. Next, Olympia's image floated into his brain. Wife material? Totally. Mother material? Possibly. She might have hidden nurturing talents. People couldn't be taken at face value. If there was one thing life had taught him, it was that fact.

Sophie was an obvious nurturer. However, Sophie already had someone in her life. Beau was keeping her from him, whoever he was. Boss or not. *Who is he?* None of his business, that's who.

There were still a lot of good times ahead, as long as Sophie stuck around. She'd never answered yes or no about a family pool party. But, why did she freak out every time he brought up building a fire?

Anyway. Maybe Beau should introduce Olympia to the kids. Just see what happened. Well—make that *after* he'd finished submitting their proposal to the Department of Defense.

Chapter 11

Sophie

The Cabots and Sophie walked wide-eyed into the Hot Cocoa Festival, the air a mix of steam and chocolate and Christmas amazingness. "Wow. It's so pretty in here." Sophie's breath caught.

The gymnasium of the Sugarplum Falls Recreation Center was draped with strands of Christmas lights, peeking through a deep indigo covering above to make it look like a night sky. It was Sophie's first time in the building, but even she could tell there'd been a miraculous transformation. It was obviously a decorating feat.

"Whoa!" Mac said. "Where are we?"

"We're in the gym where you take Tae Kwon Do," Beau said over the jolly music.

"Nuh-uh." Mac's neck craned to look around. "I think we're in a cartoon."

Magic twinkled all around, and the air smelled like cocoa and popcorn, Sophie's favorite. What a great choice for an annual Cabot Family Christmas Tradition. Beau should bring the kids to this every year.

The Hot Cocoa Festival pulsed with steamy, chocolaty energy. Sophie wandered the aisles of booths and games at Beau's side, each of them keeping a tight grip on one child's hand. Divide and conquer was tonight's game plan.

Adele pointed to a booth. "Wow! Look. Can I do that? I want to hit an elf on the head with a whacker." She wriggled out of Sophie's grasp and raced toward the holiday-themed version of the garden-pest carnival game.

Mac followed just as fast. "I'm going to beat you."

Beau reached after Mac but only caught air. He looked at Sophie. "I guess we'd better ..." They jogged after the kids. "You and I both know they're not trustworthy in public."

That was an understatement, but actually, it turned out fine. Fun, even. They whacked elves; Mac won that contest. They raced toy reindeer stuffed animals on toboggans down little ice luges; Beau's was fastest. They blew peppermint-scented bubblegum bubbles; Adele's was biggest.

All game booths paused activities while a local couple sang a romantic duet, and then the organizers ran a date-setup game for singles in the town, drawing names from a Santa hat. Poor suckers. Thank all the mall and department store Santas that Sophie didn't have to face that humiliation. Once it was over, everything swung back into action, though.

Sophie tested every flavor of cocoa her stomach could hold.

"Which one do you vote for?" Beau asked. "Should we each vote, or put in one group vote?"

"I'm voting for the salted caramel cocoa." Adele sat with four cups lined up in front of her spot at the picnic table. "Except I really like the one with cinnamon, too." She looked so grown up while executing her decision-making process. "It's a toss-up."

"A toss-up, huh?" Beau tugged lightly on her braid. "What about you, Mac?"

"Easy." He slammed back a cup of cocoa. "Reindeer droppings flavor."

Of course he'd pick that. "Somebody was pandering to boy-humor here tonight." Sophie held her hands around her warm cup. "What about you?"

"Yeah, Daddy? What kind did you like?"

"I liked the one with cayenne."

"No!" Adele hollered. "That was so spicy! It burned my tongue."

"All of them burned my tongue," Mac said, with his tongue out. "I can't even taste anything anymore." Which would explain his choice of favorite flavor.

"Some like it hot," Sophie said, lifting a brow at Beau—but then letting it fall just as quickly when an image hit her of what that nanny Gemma might have looked like flirting with Beau right before getting canned.

"Sounds like we each have to vote," adult-toned Adele declared. "What about you, Aunt Sophie? Which one will you vote for?"

"Peppermint, I think."

"Some like it cool," Beau murmured, looking too pointedly into Sophie's eyes until she had to look away. "Okay, gang. Let's cast our ballots!" He gathered up their cups and they went to the voting boxes.

While the kids climbed the candy-cane tower, Sophie and Beau took a breather and watched the couples dance who'd been matched during the mayor's dating game.

"So, do you think the Sugarplum Falls mayor played it straight?" Sophie asked. "Or do you think she cheated and just called the names of couples she wanted to line up together?"

"Like, is she some kind of sneaky matchmaker? I don't know. I'm just glad I managed to escape her crosshairs."

"Why, Captain Beau Cabot." Up walked a middle-aged woman with a gleam in her eye. "I can see now why you wriggled out of my grasp for the date-line-up festivities tonight." She ran an appraising eye over Sophie, nodding as if the vision of Sophie satisfied her immensely. "Yes, indeed. Quite a catch. Where have you been hiding her?"

"Mayor Lang." Beau cleared his throat and shifted his weight uncomfortably. "This is my sister-in-law, Sophie Hawkins."

"Sophie, huh? Sister-in-law. I see." The mayor nodded as if she was piecing together a puzzle. "That explains the resemblance. Uncanny, isn't it? Well, other than the …" Mayor Lang indicated her own chest. "Sophie's is *much* more impressive than your ex-wife's." She cackled a little too loudly. Like the Wicked Witch of the West, but with a nicer edge to it.

Sophie curled inward. *My chest is not that big.* She glanced down, and then at Beau. Beau was appraising it, too. Ugh. *Thanks a lot, mayor lady.*

The mayor turned back to Beau. "Plus, no nasty tattoos on Tracey two-point-oh. Appears you definitely traded up, Beau Cabot."

"We're not—" Beau waved his hand almost violently. "She's my—"

"I heard you." Mayor Lang held up a palm to silence him then turned to Sophie. "Hang onto this one. Oh, and by the way, he's told you about Sugarplum Falls, right? That it's a third-date-kiss type of town?" An exaggerated wink followed. "Let me be the first to wish you joy." She turned and marched triumphantly away.

Beau scrubbed a hand down his face. "I'm so sorry, Sophie. The mayor is …"

"First we're ideal parents, now this." If only at least one of the beverages in this room were cold to soothe the heat creeping up her neck and face. "Don't worry about it. I'm used to the comparisons to Tracey's appearance by now."

Until Tracey went off the rails, running off with rock stars and ruining her perfect skin, the comparisons had never been in Sophie's favor, even in the bra-size area. *I should probably mind. I should probably defend my sister. But she doesn't deserve it.*

"I've been her sister all my life, you know."

"Not that." He pushed his eyebrows together. "Let's just say Mayor Lang isn't known for her tact when it comes to single people's relationships."

Sophie laughed out loud. "I'm pretty sure I could have guessed that."

He looked at her earnestly, as if he was begging her to forgive. "So, you're not upset?"

That yet another stranger had assumed Sophie was together with the man of her dreams, and that a wannabe matchmaker had told Beau that having Sophie at his side was trading up? Hardly.

"I got to the top of the tower first!" Adele launched into Beau's arms. "But Mac beat me down."

Mac walked up, tears brimming. "I fell."

"Oh, dear. It's probably about time to wind up our time at the festival," she whispered to Beau. He gave a curt nod.

They played one more game of beanbag toss, where Mac won a stuffed snowman, and handed it to Sophie, who crouched down to receive it.

"This is for you, Aunt Sophie," he said, beaming, and giving her a hug. "I won it for you because you made today awesome."

Sophie hugged him to her heart. "Thanks, Mac." She kissed his head. "You made it awesome, too."

When she stood up, Beau was gazing at her again, but she couldn't read its meaning, although it warmed her to a dangerous degree. He shouldn't look at her like that, not after denying so vehemently to the mayor that they were together. Not after telling Sophie that he'd fired Gemma, a previous child-care provider, for showing an interest in him. It wasn't fair. Or nice.

Because—chances were, if he looked at any woman that way, he was asking her to throw herself at him with energy and determination.

Ah, case in point: the energy and determination displayed on the face of the woman stalking her way toward them in the sexy black cat suit. Well, or something like it. It was a black turtleneck and jeans, and it happened to hug the woman to advantage. Plus, with that swoop of eyeliner, she could get the role of Catwoman in any superhero production.

Yeah, she still strode toward Beau, not taking her eyes off him.

Really, could a person look more out of place at a town family Christmas event? And yet, the woman obviously didn't care about fitting in. Confidence whooshed in a giant arc around her, like she knew how much she stood out— and loved it.

"Well, Beau Cabot. You're off-duty, it would seem." She batted her eyes at Beau, almost as if her blinks were choreographed. "Who's this?" She swept a gaze over Sophie, her upper lip setting in place. "New nanny?"

Why didn't I think to wear my battle uniform? Why am I in a pilly, formless Christmas sweatshirt decorated with different colors of mittens and cats at this moment?

"Olympia Barron, this is Sophie Hawkins, my sister-in-law."

"Pleased to meet you," Sophie white-lied.

"I thought she looked familiar. A near-copy of the original." She gave Sophie another cursory once-over with her eyes then dismissed her. "What about our deadline, Beau?"

Beau tugged at the place where his scarf met his throat. "I'm making progress. My kids needed a family outing." He nodded toward the stage where that awful date setup had happened a few minutes ago. "I thought Mayor Lang would have tapped you to be on her list for the dating hat setup."

Like she owned him, or wanted to, this Olympia feline ran a long finger down his cheek. "Oh, Beau. I might have let her manipulate me into it if you had, too."

Well! Sophie stifled a gasp. So that's how it was with this woman. *How could Beau resist her?* One answer: he probably couldn't.

Then, in a surprise offensive, Olympia turned to Sophie. "You're wonderful to give Beau all this extra time at the office with me. He told me about the sacrifice you're making for Tazewell this month. Thank you." She bobbed her head in a gracious nod of thanks. "And I hear the kids are nuts about you."

Adele stepped between them, like a little human shield. "We love Aunt Sophie."

Mac piped up, at his usual too-loud volume. "Yep! She taught us to make cookies and pizza pockets. And daddy did this one move at family charades the other night, and—" Mac made the Marilyn Monroe figure move with his hands, but his remaining words were muffled, due to Beau's hand being clamped over the loud mouth. "Hey," he said when released. "I couldn't breathe." He turned and gave Beau a little punch.

Ooh. Not good. Sophie caught her breath, attempting not to cringe or imagine the consequences later.

Olympia raised a brow. "Charming children." She looked back at Beau. "See you Monday? We'll call that T-minus seven days and counting, yes?"

Beau murmured something in the affirmative, and the woman slinked away. How could someone walk like that and not fall down? Half her movement was left-to-right, or more. At least as much as it was forward. Waste of energy.

Well, maybe. It seemed to be creating energy among the male populace of the crowd. Many, many pairs of eyes followed Olympia What's-her-name through the winter wonderland of the Hot Cocoa Festival.

Whoa. Sophie had to hang onto Adele's scarf's end to even process that woman. Sophisticated, alluring, irresistible. Plus, Olympia clearly had her sights set on Beau. And they worked together. What if that was the woman Beau chose to fill his life with once Sophie left?

It would make perfect sense if he selected her as a wife.

But what about the kids?

The hair on the back of Sophie's neck stood up.

Why do I suddenly want to go to war?

On the way out to the SUV, Beau said, "How about after church tomorrow you and I scout for a Christmas tree out on the grounds?"

"Sounds nice." She might have answered absently, considering all the emotions crowding to the forefront of her mind. They inserted the kids and closed the back doors. "Should we take the kids? They'll have definite ideas of what tree they want."

"Oh, I'm sure they will. Ceiling scrapers or they need not apply." Beau kind of smiled—but was it due to a memory of that Olympia woman's attention? It could be. Any man would be basking in the glow of it for hours. "It's better if we plan ahead, *guide* them to the right tree."

"I see." So, he'd thought this out. Or else he'd learned from past experience. Tree-argument-disaster was easy to picture, considering the forceful personalities of Sophie's two favorite little people on earth. "I can probably attend, in a consulting capacity, since you're obviously the expert. Maybe we could put on a movie for them while we scout."

"Like a rainbow unicorn Christmas movie, if one exists," Beau said, and now he genuinely smiled. "And you and I could *miss* it while we're out."

"I'll look forward to tree-scouting even more."

Unfortunately, after church the next day, Beau disappeared into his office for an hour. When he emerged, it was plain as day that something happened with Tazewell, and he had one of those deer-in-the-headlights panics written all over his body.

"I'm sorry, Sophie." He sounded genuinely overwrought, tugging at the white shirt and tie he'd worn to church. "I promised and I'm flaking out."

"Please. Of all things, don't worry about this." She brushed it aside, as she handed him his deluxe peanut butter sandwich from when he'd missed lunch with the kids. Sure, she'd have liked to hike in the forest with him, but it was hardly pressing. "We'll tree-hunt another day. For tomorrow, something relaxing. Maybe that swim?"

As long as the water won't be cold.

Beau's shoulders dropped, and he exhaled audibly. "Yes. That would be great." He took a bite of the sandwich, chewing like he'd just been fed ambrosia instead of a PB&J. "The mineral hot springs water is probably exactly what I'll need. And the kids will love it. I don't let them swim unless I supervise."

And he'd been too busy, the unspoken guilt crossed his brow.

But *mineral hot springs* ricocheted back and lodged in her consciousness. "It's hot water in the pool? I'm really looking forward to this." She might be beaming. "We can play Marco Polo, and maybe make it Christmas-related. Like shouting *Santa, Claus! Santa, Claus!* instead." She made it sound like a call and an echo.

Okay, now she sounded silly.

Beau didn't seem to mind. "It's a plan." For a split second, he looked like he might lean in and give her another one of his signature awkward hugs, but he blinked a couple of times and then turned to go. "I have to head to Tazewell. See you in the morning?"

"Sure." She'd make him a nourishing breakfast. Something with protein. Maybe there were foods that fight stress. But then, after his SUV disappeared down the drive, a horrifying thought dawned: *I didn't bring a swimsuit.*

***

The swim activity didn't happen the next day, or the next. Sophie hunted online for a swimsuit, but everywhere she looked, they were on back-order or out of season. Or just plain ugly. *I don't want to wear an ugly suit. Not in front of Beau.* Finally, she ordered one. It was awful, but it was a swimsuit.

But the swim wasn't the only activity that got postponed. The Beau-and-Sophie private hike into the woods to choose a tree just got shoved aside altogether.

Instead, on Monday, Beau gave them twenty minutes of a Christmas craft with green-dyed popsicle sticks and red construction paper.

On Tuesday, Beau cut down a tree and hauled it to the house, where they set it up, filling the room with the scent of boughs and holidays. No time to decorate it, just to set it up.

On Wednesday after school, Sophie had made one last-ditch effort to more-or-less guilt Tracey into talking with her kids.

Tracey. Ugh.

At first, when Sophie got her to pick up the phone, Tracey made excuses to Sophie. She was busy. She had had a long day.

"They're your kids, Tracey. Your son and daughter. What could be more important?"

"Fine," Tracey huffed. "Fine. Let me talk to Adele."

Handing the phone off to her, however, felt like passing a live grenade to a child. Sophie didn't eavesdrop, but she did hold her breath. *Please let Tracey listen when Adele tells her about the spelling bee.*

About three minutes later, Adele came back into the room, beaming. "I told her everything."

"Great." Sophie waited for details. Adele was good for details.

"She told me about New York and somebody gross called Nee-Row."

Uh-oh. Maybe Tracey had dominated the conversation. Sophie wouldn't put it past her. And why would Adele know Nero was gross? Kids did have a sixth sense about people sometimes. "Okay. What did you tell her?"

"I told her about the spelling bee and the Hot Cocoa Festival, and the light show on the waterfall, and that we're going to decorate our Christmas tree at Turtledove Place, and about swimming with you and Daddy, and caroling and cookies, and building Mr. Snowman and Mrs. Snowman. She said it sounded like we were having a great Christmas without her."

Then Adele frowned.

"What's wrong?"

"I don't know. I don't think Mommy is having a good Christmas."

Huge sigh. Probably not. *Mommy made some choices, kid.* "I bet she was glad to hear you and Mac are having a good Christmas, though."

Adele re-lit, like one of those trick birthday candles. "Yep! We are. It's the best Christmas ever. I'd say best-est, but that's not a word."

Cha-ching. Mission accomplished! Sophie couldn't wait to tell Beau. He had a lot to be proud of in that answer.

That night, it was family tree-decorating time. Sophie straightened boughs, fluffing them, and pulling little spiders off. Trees straight from the forest usually brought creatures along. She poured Seven-Up into the water at the base of the tree, since that's what her grandma had always done—said it gave the tree the sugar it needed to keep its needles longer.

This one only needed a few days of needles. Christmas was less than two weeks away.

And I'll be leaving. Unless …

Beau tromped down the stairs, his arms laden with boxes.

"You found them!" Sophie looked up from the puzzle she and Adele were putting together. One huge red box in Beau's arms was labeled *Christmas ornaments.* "Where were they?"

"On the top shelf of a storage room over the garage—of the master bedroom."

A place Sophie wouldn't have ventured into to look for them. "Okay, kids. It's time." She ran to Beau's side and took the box. "Are there more?"

"Are there!" He laughed drily. "This is Mary Tazewell we're talking about. And her mother, Pearl Smith. There are more decorations than Walmart and Target put together."

"I'll help." Sophie handed Adele a box of non-breakable ornaments. "Put these on the tree anywhere you like. I'll help your dad bring down more."

"More!" Mac shouted. "Yeth!"

Yeah, Sophie needed to get started on that right after school.

When she and Beau reached the second floor hallway, she stepped closer, ooh. Right into aftershave range. "I'm going to start working with Mac after school tomorrow on his S sounds. Does he have a favorite treat that might motivate him?"

It was standard operating procedure as a therapist to involve the parents ahead of time.

"Honestly, I think you'd know better than I would." Beau gazed at her. "I can't tell you how much it means to me to have you here for the kids, Sophie. Have I told you that lately?"

Never. But he could tell her all day long, especially if he let his aftershave ensconce her and his compliments warm her from head to toe.

"I feel honored to be able to be part of their lives."

They retrieved the ornaments, and downstairs they worked for a good hour, placing them all up and down the tree. Beau, on a ladder, was in charge of the upper layers, since indeed, the chosen tree had stretched higher when it came inside than it had looked in its forest home.

Boy howdy, but watching a man wield a chainsaw? And fell a tree? Shoosh, she fanned herself just remembering.

Adele waved an empty ornament box at Sophie, creating a second breeze. "Are you hot, Aunt Sophie?"

Yep. Because your dad is, kid.

"What are all these?" Mac pulled out a cardboard box. "Airplanes?"

Beau's head snapped toward Mac. "Airplanes? Really?" Beau jumped off the second rung of the ladder. "Hey. I haven't seen these in a long time." Gingerly, he took them from their package, one by one. "Cool," he said under his breath.

Something magical was happening.

Beau looked like he had just climbed into a time machine trip to thirty years ago. Wonder sparkled all around him.

"She kept them." He placed one on the tree, and then spun its propeller. "Osprey, takes off like a helicopter but it converts to a turboprop." He hung it on the tree and then reached for the Huey.

Sophie tried not to stare, but it was hard.

"Dad's helicopter." Beau worked his jaw, turning the Iroquois model over in his hands. "Utility chopper. U.S. Army commissioned tens of thousands of them, beginning in nineteen fifty-nine for medical evacuation in Asia. Dad flew one in the eighties for the same purpose, but in Central America."

Dad, he'd said, almost tightly. Beau didn't put the Huey on the tree. He set it aside.

"Is that a C-124 Globemaster?" Sophie reached for one of the cargo planes still in its box. "Did you make these all yourself?"

"Uh, yeah." Beau looked up. "How did you know it was a Globemaster?"

Sophie shrugged. "I've always liked planes." Which he should remember. It's what had brought them together in the first place.

Beau squinted a moment. "You were one sharp cookie."

"Uh, thanks?" Was *sharp cookie* a good thing? "But obsessed is more the word for it. I recreated the spotter plane charts with the silhouettes of U.S. planes from World War I, World War II, and the Viet Nam War supposedly as an extra credit project for my high school history class—but that was a sham, since I'd already memorized them when I was ten."

"Man, that was a long time ago." Beau rubbed his chin. "Did we talk about the AT-6 training plane?" When she nodded he said, "You and I kind of got carried away talking about the T-6 trainer and the T-53A prop-engine training jets until your school teacher had to interrupt us so the kids could go to lunch."

And so Sophie could go to the orthodontist. With Tracey. "I was such a nerd about planes."

"I thought it was cool. You were the only one who cared in the whole class."

"In the whole school, you mean. Everyone else only cared about video games. I apologize for my entire generation."

"I love video games!" Mac yelled. In addition to the lisp, they might want to check the kid's hearing. So much yelling. Please. "Let's stop this and play games."

Sophie and Beau exchanged looks.

"Really, the tree has enough decorations now," she said, and the words were like a starting gun at a horse race for the kids. They shot out of the gate, away from the mess of boxes and tissue in a flash.

"They aren't evenly spaced," he said, frowning and putting away the ladder.

"That's the beauty of a family tree—the chaos."

"Okaaaay." They began tidying up. "Did I tell you, you look good in red?"

She did? She pressed the fabric of her red t-shirt. Ooh, it had slid upward a little at her waist. Beau's eyes strayed there. Was her skin showing? Oh, dear.

Beau swallowed, his Adam's apple rising and falling and causing Sophie's stomach to flutter. He cleared his throat. "Um, oh. Right. I have good news. Did I tell you?"

She'd better stop staring at his lips, but he was moistening them, and it was a problem. "Is it work-related?" she managed.

"Uh-huh." He blinked a few times as if snapping back to attention. "I think I've gotten past a block I was up against at work. With luck, I'll be able to submit a proposal Tazewell Solutions has been preparing for over the past three years. If I can get it submitted, I think we're a shoo-in for the government contract."

"Great news. Government contract, huh? Is that what you've been working so hard on?" He hadn't been secretive, even though he hadn't been forthcoming.

"It's been a long-term project. We'll know by the end of the year whether we're successful. If we receive it, it will set the company up for ... a generation, I'm thinking."

Wow. Lucrative. Sophie looked at the ornament box in her hands. "And if you don't get it?"

"If not, well, let's just say I'd be looking at re-enlistment for active duty."

Oh! But, the kids! They'd be uprooted, and they'd already endured so much upheaval. "Is there anything I can do to help you prevent that?" Her heart nearly leapt at him. "I'm here for you. Anything."

Beau rubbed at the muscles on his shoulder. "I don't know."

Sophie watched his hands, but she set down the box and walked around behind him. "Here. I can at least help you with that." Grasping his shoulders, which were—holy cow, so broad—she turned him around, stood on the bottom rung of the ladder and placed him in front of her. "May I?"

"Would you?"

With the base of her palm, she pressed into the muscle. "This is like a rock." But not in the good way she'd normally mean. It was so tight it was like it had petrified.

"I know, right?" He groaned, either in pain or relief, she couldn't say. "I don't do a lot of tree chopping most of the time. If it's already this bad, I hate to think what it will be like tomorrow."

Sophie pulled aside the collar of his shirt so she could get to his bare skin. *Don't think about that. He's in pain.* She kneaded his muscle, looking for the pain center. It had to be there somewhere. "This isn't all from chopping down a tree. It's stress-related."

He exhaled and slowly his shoulders fell. "My stress will go down in a month."

Yeah, or else it would shoot upward. "Try to think about happy things."

She pressed circles into the tight area and the muscles surrounding it. "Do you want some ibuprofen?" She explored his shoulder muscle until—there. There was the hard knot's full depth. With her thumbs, she created a circular pressure.

"No, just keep on … right. Right there." He sighed, as if she'd just hit a release-button. "You have amazing hands."

"Thank you." Matt had asked for a backrub once and said Sophie was the best. "I don't know why, but I have a sense for where someone's pain is. It's like my fingers work until they find it."

"I believe that with all my heart. And shoulders." He moaned. "Sophie, you are …"

What? She was what? In love with him, just like she'd been since they'd talked planes when she was too young to be in love but couldn't help herself?

"Incredible," he finished.

She realized she'd stopped working the area. "Me?" she whispered.

Beau stepped away. He turned around, just a breath from her face, her elevated spot on the ladder making their faces the same height.

He edged closer. If she hadn't had the ladder behind her to keep her steady, she would have lost her balance, would have fallen for him in the literal sense. But it kept her upright.

He placed his hands on her hips, his fingers pressing into the skin of her back, and pulling her ever-so slightly toward him. His lips parted, and Sophie's breath caught. *He's going to kiss me.* She couldn't breathe. This moment she'd dreamed for ages was here, it was now. And he smelled like pine wood and peppermint and manliness.

Sophie whispered, moistening her lips, when—

"Aunt Sophie! You have to see this part on Captain Firestarter!" Adele and Mac tumbled over each other to get her attention.

She sprang back from Beau's gaze, after being completely *engrossed* in Captain Cabot and the fire he was starting inside her. Beau rubbed the back of his neck as the plane ornaments suddenly became the most interesting thing in his world.

"Uh, sure, kids." Sophie stepped down from the ladder, and followed them into the living room. She didn't glance back at Beau.

What if he was watching her, but not with longing. Instead, what if he was looking at her with embarrassment at his mistake? Because a kiss between Beau and Sophie would definitely be spelled m-i-s-t-a-k-e.

***

A few mornings later, after snatches of family time each day between Beau's working stints, including over the weekend, Sophie bundled the kids up, made some lunches, and sent them to school. Yes, she should study, now that Vronky had sent the package with all Sophie's textbooks. Yes, her boards loomed. Yes, her whole future rode on whether she passed that test.

However, she had a much bigger problem taking up all the real estate in her brain.

Her swimsuit hadn't come in the mail yet. She checked her email for the delivery notification.

Not sent yet. They hadn't even mailed it!

Sugarplum Falls had better have a swimsuit for sale. The family swim could hit her at any time. Plus, she needed something truly distracting to keep her mind off that near-kiss, which she never should have allowed to happen. It was almost as if there'd been a fire in the grate stealing her brain cells. Geez.

Downtown, Sophie found a parking place outside that truly charming bookstore where she'd first asked for directions when she came to Sugarplum Falls. Talk about prodigious. A bookstore was just what she'd been thinking about for gifts. Maybe they'd have a good selection. *I need something just right. For him.*

It drew her in, despite her main goal of swimsuit or bust. She'd shop for books and then ask for swimsuit shopping advice. The Millikens she had met before probably knew the answer to that question, as well.

"Hello," the familiar face of Mrs. Milliken called from behind the cash register's counter. "Merry Christmas. Welcome to Angels Landing. Browse all you like. We're here if you need. Oh, hi. I remember you, lovely young lady. Did you ever find Beau Cabot and Turtledove Place?"

"Sure did."

"I knew you would. Easy peasy. Happy shopping." She went back to polishing something, and Sophie breathed the lovely scents of cinnamon and cherry candles—and books. Bookshops always had that homey, comforting smell.

Wandering the shelves, she picked up and replaced several volumes. No, not quite right.

"Hi. And Merry Christmas." A good-looking man in a sweater and horn-rimmed glasses approached her a few minutes later. She'd seen him somewhere before. "I'm Sam Bartlett, the owner of Angels Landing. Is there something in particular you need? We're a little low on inventory of some genres right now, due to"—he grimaced—"unavoidable circumstances. However, we have a good selection in others."

Sophie couldn't help wondering what the grimace was about. "Militaria?" she asked. "I don't know exactly what I'm looking for, but that's the direction I want to go for this gift."

"Are you buying for your father?" Mr. Bartlett led her down a long aisle toward the back. "Just asking because a lot of daughters choose military history books for their dads. It can be a truly personal gift."

"Um, not this time." Telling him it was for her brother-in-law would sound strange. Especially after he'd referred to the gift book as *truly personal*. "Oh, this is great." Sam had deposited her in an alcove made of shelves, and every book looked like a potential match. "Thank you."

"Sure. If you need anything, holler."

"Children's section? For when I'm finished here?"

"Toward the front, right behind the front window display." He gave a little salute and left Sophie to her browsing, and she immersed herself in the surprisingly good selection of volumes on military history, biographies, and so forth.

Finally, she settled on the perfect military book, feeling all tingly inside. *He won't mind I'm getting him a gift, will he? It won't be awkward, right?*

Then, she headed to the front of the store and the children's section. Oh, this was where the real fun began. Book after nostalgic book leapt from the shelves into her arms. Whatever weaknesses Mom might have suffered from as a mother, reading aloud to Sophie as a child hadn't been one of them.

Her arms ended up loaded down with old friends. It was going to be delightful to cuddle together on the couch with picture books and chapter books and longer novellas full of funny characters and endearing illustrations.

Time flows differently in bookstores. The church bells chimed twelve o'clock—and her stomach growled for lunch. Whoa, noon? Really? She hadn't accomplished the most pressing and potentially impossible task, and she'd need to meet Mac from the early bus soon. Yikes!

And the family swim was tonight.

"All of these?" Mrs. Milliken asked, and a pair of reading glasses dangled from a chain around her neck. "So, how were things up at Turtledove Place?"

"Pretty good." Not great, considering the lady of the house had abandoned her children. "Hanging in there."

"So, you're staying there? Nice. I haven't been to visit in years. Do you like the house? What about the grounds? The view is spectacular."

"Especially at sunset. I'm so glad my niece and nephew get to grow up somewhere so perfect."

Mrs. Milliken nodded slightly, as if filing away that informational tidbit. "Pearl Smith, what a gracious woman. She and her husband were the original owners, you know. Captain Cabot's grandmother. Lucky woman. Mr. Smith left a great legacy."

"The house is great."

"Yes, but I was talking about the ability to love a woman. Now, that's what I consider a legacy." Mrs. Milliken rang up the purchases, while Sophie could do nothing but consider what that statement could mean. "There are going to be some very happy children in your life."

"I hope so. They're my world." *Even though their mother had abandoned them and apparently wanted nothing to do with them.* Sophie had to try, at least.

"Would you like these gift-wrapped?"

"Aw, no. Wrapping is half of the gift." Sophie accepted the receipt. "Thank you, though. Oh, by the way. I find myself in need of a swimsuit."

"Swimsuit!" Mrs. Milliken gawked. "You're not doing one of those mad-brained polar bear plunge things, are you? Please say no. Sugar Lake is *not* meant for anything but ice fishing this time of year."

Not a freezing chance. "Turtledove Place has a pool." Not that she'd seen it yet.

"Oh, right. The hot springs pool. I'd forgotten." Mrs. Milliken smiled and handed her a receipt. "Are you staying there long?"

"Probably just until Christmas." Absolutely just until Christmas. "I'm helping out with the children for the holidays."

"Oh, aren't you wonderful!" Mrs. Milliken rested a dry, cool hand on Sophie's. "Mrs. Smith would have loved having children living in the house. A little nest for her fledgling grandchildren."

A long pause ensued, and Sophie didn't know how to fill it. Finally, Mrs. Milliken came back to earth. "Oh, but yes. The sporting goods store has swimsuits year-round. Sugarplum Sports, down the block on the left. If I recall the rumor correctly, they might even have a candy cane-striped one for the holidays, if you're that type of person." Mrs. Milliken inspected Sophie closer. "I get the sense you are—since you value the activity of wrapping gifts."

"Thank you. I'll take that as a compliment."

"It's a high one. Christmas is special."

Agreed. Sophie lugged her heavy purchase to her car.

Ugh. Swimsuit shopping. She couldn't face it just yet.

She stopped in at The Cider Press for a hot spiced apple cider to go. Mmm, it tasted perfectly fruity and spicy, and it warmed her all the way through. And the girl serving the cider was really cute, sighing over the Korean drama playing on three different TV sets in her shop at the same time.

Then she darted into Sugarbabies Bakery for a small stack of gingerbread men from a nice woman with a broad grin named Mrs. Toledo before heading to face the swimsuit music. It didn't matter who you were, swimsuit shopping was not for the female faint of heart.

Candy cane swimsuit? Really?

It turned out, Sugarplum Sports did not have the candy cane-striped swimsuit in anything but men's trunks so large that they'd cause her a problem if she wore them, even with a piece of rope tied around the waistband to keep them up.

In a way, that was a blessing.

However, they also didn't have any one-piece suits in her size. Or in almost anyone's size. Everything was clearance-awful and skimpy. Sophie had always been a one-piece swimsuit girl—high neckline, low on the thigh, lots of coverage to protect against the sun, since her skin was pretty much china-doll white.

"Do you have any other suits in the back?" she asked the clerk feebly. "Something for, maybe, lap swimming, competition racing?" Those were always reliable, and this was a sporting goods place, after all.

"Not until spring." The clerk popped her gum. "Sorry, lady. This is what we got." She went back to reading her phone. "You'd look real good in those, though. If I had what you've got, I'd probably walk around town all year in that stringy one."

The stringy one! It didn't have enough fabric to wrap a Hershey's Kiss with, let alone Sophie's whole physique.

She flung the garments along the metal rack, the hangers making a metallic zing of *No, no, no*. Oh, maybe? She stopped on one. Royal blue. Ugh, it wasn't much better, but it was the only one with any yardage to speak of. Oh, and look. It was in her size—the only suit in her size, actually. What luck. Ugh. She held it up to herself, since there was no way she'd be trying it on in the dressing room and humiliating herself in semi-public. It would either work when she put it on at Turtledove Place, or … or she'd just swim fully clothed.

Wonderful idea to plant in Adele and Mac—that they could jump in their pool anytime wearing school clothes.

Considering swimming as a family had been Beau's one big family-activity request since the charades debacle, could Sophie really shoot it down? No. Not a chance. It was this suit or nothing.

Uh, no. Whoops. *Do not let your brain go down that path.*

"Are you all right? You just turned really red." The clerk handed Sophie the bag and receipt. "Do you need some fresh air?"

Did she ever.

Chapter 12

Beau

Beau adjusted in his seat at his desk at Tazewell. Nothing was coming to him, still. This blankety-blank application was driving him to the brink of insanity.

He'd think about something else. Just for a minute.

And he'd already done far too much thinking about that almost-kiss with Sophie while they decorated the tree. If he closed his eyes, he could still picture the tilt of her face, the pink of her lips, feel the soft whisper of her breath against his skin—which combined to raise his heart-rate even now, a few days later. Nothing pacifying about that memory.

Model planes usually calmed him, so he turned around in his chair and examined the collection on his shelf that he'd assembled over the years. Some he'd personally made, others he'd found in shops or online. He reached for the model of the T-53A prop-engine he'd trained on years ago, when he almost became a pilot.

Not a helicopter. Helicopters were Dad's thing. He spun the propeller, toying with it for a minute or two, picturing the ground and trees and ocean passing beneath him.

Picturing the conversation he'd had with Sophie about planes while they decorated the tree. How did she know so much about every single plane he liked? It was a turn-on. For sure. But not as big of a turn-on as having her work the demon knot out of his shoulder.

He rolled his head around. Ah, it was gone.

Until he looked at the computer again, the blank text box practically blinking at him. *I have to get past this next section.* Blocked, still. And his mind wasn't getting clearer. Just fuzzier with thoughts of Sophie and her magical hands of healing.

The kids! Yeah. He could think about Mac and Adele. They'd been so much easier to handle since Sophie came. He actually enjoyed them again. Maybe they could do something fun together after work tonight. *The swim.* Yeah. Wasn't that on the schedule? What he'd really like was a fire. If he could sit in front of a fire, then his mind would finally unlock. And if Sophie would work on the re-forming knot in his neck, it would be even better for his psyche.

Why was Sophie so averse to the idea of cooking marshmallows over a fire? Roasted marshmallows were the food of happiness, of both summer and holidays. They were the perfect, one-bite treat. Well, maybe tonight after the family swim, he could finally convince her.

Yeah, no question, Beau needed a fire. It would help his soul unwind. Something about the flame, the radiant light and heat, always helped him think better. And while he did want to brainstorm Christmas traditions with Sophie, even more he needed the mellowing of his mind a fire could give to help him come up with a solution to this blocked section on his application.

I can't get this wording. Until I get this wording, the government form won't let me fill out the rest of the application. Bureaucracy and forms. A pox on them. They were thwarting his life's progress, threatening to sink Pops's company and life's work. And he'd trusted Beau.

"Hey, man." At his door stood Jordan McNair, owner of Frosty Ridge Lodge. "How's it going?"

Beau stood up to shake Jordan's hand. "Long time no see." They caught up for a minute on small talk—snowfall totals for this year's ski season, the expectations for local tourism.

"The powder snow is excellent this year. You still planning on bringing your company up for New Year's Eve?"

"I am." Assuming he could float the company financially until then.

"Big corporate dinner, dancing, entertainment, sans the boring speeches, right?"

That would depend entirely on what happened with the contract—whether it would be like a victory dance or an "and the band played on" evening while the *Titanic* that was Tazewell Solution sank its final inches into the briny deep.

"It's still on the docket. You still making prime rib for all my coworkers?"

"Do they deserve it?"

"Indeed they do." It was only Beau who wouldn't if he couldn't get this awful application submitted in time. Olympia's *T-minus* countdown clock ticked like thunder in his ears. "Looking forward to it. Glad you stopped in to confirm."

"I like the personal touch. Face to face business is always best." Jordan shifted his weight. "Hey, this is awkward, but are you bringing a date that night?"

Seriously? "Did Mayor Lang put you up to this?"

"I can't confirm or deny." Jordan laughed then shook his head. "No, she didn't, actually, but I wouldn't put it past her. She tried to rope me into that shenanigan at the Hot Cocoa Festival last weekend. I weaseled out at the last minute by claiming I needed to help my sister with her poinsettia greenhouse. She's got the local contract this year for flower placement all over town."

"Good evasive tactic." Points for creativity.

"The reason I ask about the date is we're trying to get a head count for the dinner, as well as names for the place cards. Since you wanted the tables set formally, the calligrapher on my staff is finalizing."

"Yeah. Good." It was a non-answer, and Beau knew it.

"You listed a question mark in the *plus one* RSVP, so I wasn't sure if the punctuation referred to *I don't know who yet* or a plain old *I don't know yet.*" Jordan grimaced. "I'm not here to judge, trust me. I feel your predicament daily."

"Sugarplum Falls is not a great town to be a contented bachelor. Too many matchmakers."

"I prefer to refer to them as busybodies. Mayor Lang, case in point."

They'd danced around the answer long enough, and Beau owed Jordan a response. "My question mark probably refers to *I don't know.*" Except, shouldn't he decide? It could be Tazewell's biggest ever celebration or their last hurrah.

"That's fine. I'll just leave it blank for now, with an empty seat beside you. If we have to rearrange at the last minute, we can, so no one looks

97

dateless. I only say this frankly because I've been there, man."

That was good of him. "Thanks, Jordan." Frosty Ridge really did have first class amenities. It deserved to be on the world map as a ski resort.

"Oh, and I saw you at the hot chocolate thing with someone. Who was that?" Jordan picked at his fingernails. "A new nanny, by chance? Nice looking one, if so."

"Sort of?" It was a long story, and he didn't want to go into it. "Her name's Sophie. She's family."

"Well, Sophie's got it going on. I'd have a hard time living clean with that kind of a temptation walking around."

Sophie? A temptation? *I mean, she's got a great personality, incredible hands, and I almost forgot myself and kissed her in that moment of weakness.* But—it was complicated.

"Family, huh? Is she, um, single?" Jordan seemed like he was trying to sound casual.

All the hairs on the back of Beau's neck stood up. His skin prickled. Jordan couldn't—

"I think she's got someone back home," Beau managed. "A doctor."

There. That would turn Jordan aside. *What if Sophie really is dating a doctor?* Nah. Well, could she be? Her boyfriend could be anyone. But was her boss at the speech therapy clinic a doctor? He might be.

"Oh. Gotcha." Jordan looked glum. "Hey, see you on New Year's Eve, man. Merry Christmas."

Jordan left Beau puzzling. Sophie had it going on, huh? Sophie. Young, perfect-skinned Sophie. Too young for Beau. For Pete's sake, she'd been thirteen at his wedding. She'd been barely twelve when he met Tracey.

She's not twelve anymore. Mayor Lang's inappropriate comment about Sophie's chest rang in his memory. Nothing twelve about that part of Sophie. Not that he'd been looking, not until Mayor Lang had made him look.

Okay, so there'd been moments when she might have had it *going on* for Beau, like when they washed dishes and he'd caught a bit of her shampoo's scent, or the times she gently touched his hand when he was in the dumps. At those moments, Beau had naturally experienced flashes of awareness of

Sophie's femininity.

And she definitely had a pretty face. One of the prettiest. She always had—ever since she was a little bright-eyed, intelligent girl who loved airplanes.

Come to think of it, Jordan wasn't wrong, necessarily. Maybe he was even right. The thing was, Sophie wore a lot of bulky, comfortable clothes, which made sense because she was in the trenches of kid-wrangling. Other than that day when she'd worn the white parka to play in the snow, Beau really hadn't seen her figure.

Okay, make that he hadn't allowed himself to see it. Or at least not to notice. For all the reasons. He couldn't be attracted to Sophie Hawkins. Absolutely verboten.

However, cue the dun-dun-*dun* fanfare, because his don't-notice-Sophie's-figure plan was shot to blazes during their family activity after dinner that night—planting Beau deep in Notice-Sophie-Ville.

It started innocently. Beau was watching the kids swim while Sophie changed. She was taking forever.

"Daddy, watch me! I'm swimming. I'm swimming!" Mac floated on his water wings in the shallow water. It was only a lap pool, but for a seven-year-old, Turtledove Place might as well have boasted a diving board and a pool twenty feet deep. "See? Watch me!"

Adele shouted the same thing about fifty times.

"Hey, I can only watch one of you at a time unless you swim by each other. I only have one set of eyes." Where was Sophie?

"Hey, it's Aunt Sophie!" Adele splashed like a maniac. "Get on your suit and get in."

Sophie had on a big t-shirt and a pair of oversized gym shorts. "I think I'll just watch from the deck."

"It's not family swim if you don't swim." Mac spoke as if declaring a royal edict. "You're family."

Was Sophie trembling? Even in the dim lights produced by the pool lighting, her kneecap was clearly in spasms.

"Mac's right." Beau probably shouldn't beg, but this wasn't a job for one adult. "Did you not bring a swimsuit?" Uh, probably not. Why would she know that Turtledove Place had a pool when she left to come to Sugarplum Falls from Darlington?

"I, uh, found something downtown today at the sporting goods store." She gulped and her face went red as the stoplight downtown. "They didn't have a very good selection."

It was winter. That made sense.

"Come on," Adele begged. "I want to do flips."

"Flips?" Sophie appeared to be cracking under the pressure. Good, the kid-bickering was getting to him, and he could use some divide and conquer right about now. "Are you big enough to do flips?" She kicked off her sandals.

"I'm totally big enough to do flips, but not by myself." Adele bobbed, bouncing off the bottom of the pool, making waves. "Please?"

"This suit is ... not really for *swimming,* per se. It's more for sunbathing—in San Tropez. Would it be okay if I keep my t-shirt on?" She slipped the gym shorts off and left them in a puddle, which she stepped out of. Whoa. Were her legs really that shapely? She'd been hiding them under all those cozy pajama pants she wore every day.

"Are you really going to wear your clothes in the pool?" Mac asked. "Daddy won't let us wear our clothes in the pool. Why can you?"

"There's a strict no-daytime-clothes-in-the-pool rule." Or there would be one starting right now. Beau tried to keep an eye on Mac, but his gaze kept straying to the debating Sophie still in a t-shirt. "Sorry. Family statute."

Adele's begging must have been the final straw. "I need help putting my face in the water. Please?"

Sophie winced and peeled off her t-shirt.

"Daddy's always helping Mac because he's little." Adele continued oblivious to the gloriousness that was unfolding near her.

"Hey," Mac argued like a blind person. "I'm not little."

Adele splashed the swim-ready Sophie immediately, making Sophie's skin shimmer and making Beau turn part wolf.

He shut his eyes fast. "Mac, let's see if you can float on your back." He turned away from the most sizzling thing he'd seen in person—ever.

Behind him, the water rippled. She must have gotten in with Adele, because his daughter was chattering and splashing. Meanwhile, Beau's mouth was dry, and he was more or less paralyzed by the image he'd just seen. When he closed his eyes, it was still there behind his eyelids, and he processed it.

Pretty little Sophie. Her white-blonde hair fell straight behind her shoulders. Every inch of her pale but healthy skin glistened like she'd been standing too close to a glitter factory, thanks to Adele's splash technique.

But it was the swimsuit that flipped some kind of on-switch in Beau—one that had been jammed into perma-off for years.

That royal blue bikini looked like it belonged at Palm Beach during spring break. One silver ring connected the front panels up top, and two additional silver rings rested at each hip. Those front panels were generous. Well, what they covered was. Above those hip-connector rings was a trim, narrow waist. And in the warm, dim lighting of the pool? Her pale eyes caught every flicker off the water's filtered light. She was beyond gorgeous.

If he'd ever thought she looked like her sister, he'd been dead wrong. Sophie wasn't Tracey two-point-oh. There weren't numbers high enough for comparison.

No wonder she wore the big sweatshirts. Beneath them she'd been concealing a weapon of mass destruction—of Beau's willpower.

"Watch me, Daddy!" Adele demanded, and Beau turned, but he could only look at Adele's helper, who stood on the step, waist-deep in the water.

"Looks great, sweetie." So great.

Up to now, Sophie had hovered somewhere between kid-sister and aunt-with-maternal-instincts, with the occasional *wow she's pretty and fresh* moments for him, but this sight put her squarely in another column.

"Daddy? Daddy!" Mac splashed water in Beau's face. "Did you hear what I said? I'm done floating. I want to race."

Beau knew all about racing. At least his cardiovascular system did, and it would win against any Formula One driver on the planet right now.

Sophie Hawkins. What had she done to him?

Chapter 13

Sophie

Holy cannoli *with* the little chocolate chips in the ricotta.

In all her born days of desperation-level crushing on Captain Beau Cabot, Sophie had never dreamed she'd see him both with his shirt off, looking like a more ripped version of those Italian statues—*and* looking at her with clear, unbridled desire.

Maybe she should have invested in a bikini years ago, when she first met him.

Oh, right. She'd been twelve. It wouldn't have mattered.

Tonight it had mattered. And it had been delicious. They'd stayed in the pool *much* longer than the planned twenty minutes. The kids' fingers were nothing but wrinkles by the time Sophie and Beau were done circling each other with lustful stares in the warm, enveloping water.

Upstairs in her bedroom, after bathing the kids and getting them ready for bed, she tugged on a soft cream-colored sweater she'd forgotten she brought, and a pair of also-forgotten yoga pants. The sweater was tighter than she remembered and its V-neck lower. She hadn't worn it yet this season, but she was behind on laundry, so this would have to do.

Everyone was waiting downstairs for her to join them at the marshmallow roast—which Beau had refused to take no for an answer on. "I'm the one in charge tonight," he'd said, his gaze pointedly on Sophie. "And I'm building the fire."

Oh, he'd built one in Sophie, all right. A bonfire to reach the stratosphere.

"You're sure making time for your family today," she'd said while still dripping from the pool, reaching for a towel.

It hadn't felt like family time anymore from the second she pulled off her t-shirt, though. Sophie flushed from head to toe at the memory of Beau's eyes on her terrible swimsuit. Er, except it probably hadn't been the swimsuit he'd been looking at. Then, he'd alternately averted and super-glued his gaze on her for the remainder of the evening. Several of his glances rested at the places where the rings met.

Should she bless or curse Sugarplum Sports right now?

That all depended on whether Beau took her aside tonight to tell her to leave, that she was the family equivalent of fired-as-temporary-nanny-for-shamelessly-hitting-on-the-single-dad-in-the-pool like every other Gemma or whoever that last nanny had been.

Just wearing that bikini had been playing with fire.

A million tingles started from her toes and worked their way to her scalp. Beau had looked at her—really looked at her—as a woman. *I'm definitely not a kid to him now.*

And that could be an enormous problem going forward. Because he'd never been a kid to her, and she'd never thought of him as anything but a man she wanted to love and live a life with forever.

Speaking of playing with fire, now she had to go down and face the firing squad of the fireplace—which would be taking aim at her defenses, which were down, way down, after the brain numbness that had set in when she laid eyes on Beau's impressive torso downstairs at the pool. Maybe she could stay a few minutes, roast a marshmallow, sing a song, and then leave the kid-bedtime to Beau by darting away before the mellow glow wore down all her reserves.

Except she had no desire to do so.

"That's the last marshmallow." Beau handed each kid a sweet treat. "Then bedtime prayers and sleep."

"Already?" Mac whined.

The clock chimed ten. "See? Past bedtime. Besides, Aunt Sophie and I have things to discuss."

They certainly did. For a second, alarm racked her—at the same time as the fireplace's flames drew her eyes, softening all the little frozen places at her core. "Yeah," she hummed. "Finish up, kids. We had a good swim and you must be tired."

"I'm not tired." Mac shoved the marshmallow in his mouth without roasting it.

"Me neither." Adele chomped hers, too.

"I'm invigorated." Beau ran his thumb across his lower lip, making Sophie's innards tingle. "That's it, kids. You gobbled the marshmallows."

"But we didn't roast them," Adele said through a muffled mouthful. "We have to roast them or they don't count."

"Nope. That's the breaks." He pulled each of them by the hand, almost rushing them away.

"Night-night," Sophie called as they disappeared up the stairs, leaving Sophie to war with herself.

Stay and put herself in the power of the fire, or go upstairs and always wonder?

However, Beau stopped on the first landing and silenced her inner debate. "Don't go anywhere. I'll be back in a few."

Obediently, Sophie sank back into the comforts of the sofa, inhaling the combination of the soft leather upholstery and the remnants of Beau's aftershave that lingered. Added to the burning pine in the hearth, and she was putty for the molding. With every flicker and twist of the flames, she became more and more its slave.

If Beau were to temporarily lose his mind and try anything here at the fireside, well, no guarantees on her part, other than she would have an extremely difficult time resisting. In fact, she might just refuse to resist.

Beau was single. He was fair game. He was the man she had always loved.

"Hey." Beau came down the stairs two at a time, almost like he was running to be at her side. Or so her little dreamer-heart wished. "Can I sit with you?"

"Sure." She slid a little closer to him once he settled. He didn't pull away. In fact, he leaned in. Unless she imagined it. *No, he leaned in.* Her quick breaths made her chest rise in the too-tight cream sweater.

"So, lots to talk about, right?" Beau said. "Lots and lots. For instance, how great you look in this sweater." He also eyed her legs.

"Uh-huh." She stared at his mouth. *Keep talking.* Talking with that glorious mouth begging to be kissed. Her willpower was officially toasted-marshmallow-on-a-stick-potentially-left-too-long-in-the-fire.

"Let's talk about what happened in the pool." Beau brushed a fallen strand of hair from her forehead. "And I don't mean my daughter's ability to flip."

She caught her lower lip in her teeth, willing her heart rate to slow. Yet, she couldn't break with his gaze. It owned her. "I'm really glad you built a fire. For the kids, I mean." And to create this delicious mood.

"Yeah, same," he breathed. He was staring at her mouth. "I really enjoyed our family swim."

The image of his well-exercised muscles crowded into her mind, and she pictured the two of them back in the pool's hot water, those muscles enfolding her. "Uh-huh," was all she could manage. Here on the sofa, their breaths timed, his shoulders rising and falling with hers, his gaze only leaving her eyes to make little trips to her mouth and back. She moistened her lips, and they parted slightly. He edged closer.

"Do you know you look gorgeous in the firelight?" He took her fingers and played with them one by one, killing her by inches. He lifted her index finger and pressed it to his lips. "I can't imagine why you avoid it."

Their gazes locked. The log in the fireplace crackled then popped, one collapsing onto another, mirroring the collapse of Sophie's defenses. Not that she'd bothered to put many up. Maybe she should have.

She breathed as steadily as she could. "I'm really susceptible in firelight, so you know. It's a severe weakness of mine." Oh, why had she divulged that? It was like Superman telling Lex Luthor about Kryptonite.

"Susceptible, huh?" Beau kissed the rest of her fingertips, slowly, like he needed to get to know each one by heart. "As in?"

"As in, I lose myself."

"I get that." Beau reached for her hair, taking a few strands between his fingers and brushed them across his own cheek, just like in her dream! Oh, she could die happy right now. "Totally get that." Then he switched from kissing her fingertips to the inside of her wrist.

With her free hand, Sophie curled her fingers and ran her knuckles gently down the curve of Beau's muscular neck, and it flexed beneath her touch before relaxing into it. Beau hummed, as if in supreme pleasure.

"I just forget the outside cares and live in the moment." He was very close to her now. His breath feathered against her cheek, making her emit a tiny sigh.

I'm in love with you. I've been in love with you since I was old enough to be in love.

"This is a little crazy," he whispered. "I'm not really thinking right now."

Neither was Sophie, or she might have taken that as an insult. "There are times when thinking is overrated." She let him rest his hand on her waist.

"Your eyes catch the flames. They're fire and ice." He gazed at them, and then at her mouth. "Before tonight, I hadn't really ever ..."

Thought of her as a woman? It wouldn't have been right for him to do so. But now, he could think of her in any way he liked. He could shatter her with those ache-inducing lingering stares while she wore swimwear fit for college girls, and he could grant all her lifelong-crush daydream wishes.

When his lips grazed the side of her neck, she flashed hot then cold then hot. She shivered but burned, and breathed, "I think I have a fever."

Beau pressed his lips to her throat, and then said, "Let me take your temperature." His lower lip brushed her cupid's bow. "Hot. Very hot."

Hotter than fire.

First, with touches like the sparks coming off a little candle on a birthday cake, his kiss warmed her lips, bringing them to tingling awareness. Just tiny sips of pleasure and fire. Then, he switched to sparkler wands for the Fourth of July, each tingle pricking deeper, bringing her to light and life. His mouth teased, his hands, strong, pulled her by the waist toward him. Soon, she was pressed against his firm torso, and his kiss coaxed, demanded, and required her blood to rise to dangerously high temperatures.

Oh, with these flaming kisses, Sophie was definitely playing with fire, not just physical but emotional. Beau was everything she'd wanted for so long, and now he was giving her the green light. In fact, maybe all the lights all the way down the highway were green.

A fleeting thought of tomorrow flashed a yellow light, but tonight, a yellow light was more like a choice to either slow down, or else to speed through the intersections.

Sophie stepped on the gas.

Chapter 14

Beau

Sophie's kiss was nothing like he'd expected—and nothing like Beau had ever experienced in his life. Yes, he'd shared the passion of kissing before, but not like this. Not ever like this. She was alive in his touch, and her touch in turn poured life and power and brute confidence into Beau's soul to overflowing.

He paused to breathe, and to let her catch her breath, but only for a second, and then he dove like a kamikaze pilot, ready to crash on impact. She clearly wanted him, and it'd been so long since he'd felt wanted, desired, by an intelligent, beautiful woman. It was amazing kissing Sophie Hawkins, who definitely had it going on. All this fire, and she'd been holding out on him— he'd have to get his revenge by kissing her senseless and getting her to beg for more of his kisses every day that she stayed here with him, making his life better and better.

She tilted her head back to let him explore the pristine skin of her throat with his kisses. She smelled like honey and flowers. Asters. He was going to need a good, long time on this expedition.

She moaned softly, and he pulled her tight again, every curve of her body supple in his embrace. *I need her. I need this. I want this.* With every taste of her skin he wanted Sophie more. Dating the childcare worker was a tried and true way of finding a wife—he knew. He'd watched *The Sound of Music* every Christmas with his mother. *Am I thinking of marrying Sophie?*

In this moment, he was definitely thinking of honeymooning with her. They'd absolutely go someplace with a pool.

Speaking of pools. Earlier this evening at the pool, it wasn't just his physical chemical response to Sophie's incredible swimsuit model body that had flipped a switch to *on*. Something else had ignited as well—a long latent part of Beau that he'd pretty much forgotten existed: the part that knew what he wanted and determined to go after it. The Old Beau. The Real Beau. The one who had, at some point in the nebulous past, taken a sleeping draught. Or, more accurately, had been poisoned by Tracey and left for dead.

In this kiss, Real Beau came to life and he pressed to deepen it. Sophie sighed with pleasure, and Real Beau revved the engine to speed ahead in the firelight that she admitted dampened all her defenses, making her obviously forget about whatever guy she'd left back home.

Except ... Real Beau also had a strong conscience and awareness of right versus wrong.

Sophie wasn't just some nanny he could toy with. Beau respected her. Admired her. She made him want to be the best version of himself.

Sophie's phone rang, interrupting the kiss, and she pulled away with a groan. As soon as she saw the screen, she stiffened. "I—I have to go." With one shuddering look of fear at Beau, and a second at the fire, she blinked and pressed a hand to her blazing-red cheek. "I'm so sorry, Beau. It was the fire. Fireplaces always melt my brain and make me do stupid things. I never meant to—" She turned and ran up the staircase. "Hello? Matt. Hey, there. Yeah, sure, I do miss you, of course," she said before the door to her bedroom shut.

Matt? Who was Matt? That guy she'd talked to a while ago? *He was still hanging onto her?*

More to the point, kissing Beau was a stupid thing? Since when? Nothing about the past twenty or thirty minutes felt stupid to Beau.

Well, maybe other than the fact he'd been kissing his ex-sister-in-law. But because her kiss had resurrected a fire in him he'd thought was long since buried six feet deep, even the taboo didn't matter. She was amazing.

Beau sat back and ran his thumb across the lower lip she'd worked raw, trying to regain his bearings.

No question, kissing Sophie was incredible. She'd pried loose age-old glaciers from his frozen soul. Did she really consider it a mistake?

An insidious whisper crept from the darkest part of his pain-centers. *Hawkins girls are all alike. They only want me until someone better comes along.*

Except ... Sophie and Tracey's temperaments couldn't be more different!

Beau gunned down that terrible suspicion like an enemy fighter. Sophie was sweet—with a side of secret fire. Tracey had been fire, with nothing secretly sweet. They may be sisters, but lumping Sophie together with Tracey was completely unfair.

Who is Matt?

Beau's own phone rang. "Olympia?"

"I was thinking about you, Beau."

Chapter 15

Sophie

Everyone shivered at the school bus stop—every kid, every parent, waiting for the yellow behemoth. Adele jumped up and down and batted her mittens together. Mac blew on his hands. His mittens were in his pockets, but he refused to wear them. The snow fell all around in sparkly crystals, kissing Sophie's cheeks. Just a flurry, although a blizzard was predicted for later. The world looked like fields of diamonds on acres of cotton batting.

"Can we go swimming again tonight?" Adele asked. "I loved swimming."

"No." Sophie might never be able to swim again.

"Then can we roast marshmallows again? I didn't get to roast my last one."

"No." Sophie definitely could never risk a fireplace again. Suddenly, she was shivering once more, but not as a result of the weather. "We'll think of something else. I hear there's a town Christmas play."

The kids groaned, and one of the moms in the line shook her head, like *oh, please be kind and don't put them through that.*

One of the other kids at the stop turned to Adele. "Did you put up your tree yet? My mom put hers up the day after Halloween."

"Yep," Mac said. "And then Aunt Sophie worked the kinks out of my dad."

The other moms looked at Sophie like Mac had just revealed something dirty about their household's goings-on.

"Just a kink in his neck." She held up massage fingers as if rubbing pained shoulders. The moms didn't seem to be buying it.

They probably shouldn't. Not considering what had happened on the sofa in the firelight.

Beau had left in a hurry this morning, just grabbing the bagel she'd toasted and dashing out the door with a brief thank you.

No mention of their kiss, no acceptance or rejection of her apology thereafter.

Nothing. So, maybe she was supposed to pretend like it hadn't happened. Wouldn't that be for the best?

Oblivious, Mac pinched his nose and inhaled, and his nostrils stuck together. He laughed and pointed at his misshapen face. "Look! I have a skeleton nose!"

Her phone buzzed in her pocket, but the bus was coming. She shouldn't check texts.

What if it was from Beau, though?

Hey, Sophie. My parents are thrilled you said you'd come for Christmas.

Oh, no. Matt.

Um, about that …

In her fireplace stupor last night, and in her fleeing walk of shame away from the brain-melting make-out with Beau, Sophie may have overreacted and told Matt she'd love to meet his family for Christmas, and that she'd definitely be there, no matter what.

What kind of a jerk was she?

I know, I know. You'll only be able to come if you're finished with your boards. And like I said last night, that's fine.

What all had been said last night, anyway? Sophie racked her brain to recall, but to little avail. Some people used alcohol to lose all their inhibitions and their good sense, and to forget reality. Apparently, all Sophie needed was a couple of hickory logs and she was a complete drunk for the evening. Impaired judgment to the max.

It's not just that, Matt. I'll call you after you get off work.

"We can do a dance-off tonight, but I doubt your dad will be home," Sophie promised the kids just as the bus rumbled around the corner a ways down the road. "Later on, maybe we'll watch a Christmas movie." *And I'll sit by Beau, and breathe his scent, and …*

"Can it be the one where Pegasus and the unicorn save Christmas?"

Of course, and then Sophie would concentrate on Beau and tune out the show while the kids were engrossed. "Sure. I'll make homemade popcorn."

"The kind in a bag in the microwave?" Mac asked, as if this was the ultimate treat.

"No!" Sophie recoiled. The bus was coming, its growl-snort approaching in Doppler effect. "The real stuff. You can make it on the stove."

"Can we pop it in the fireplace?"

"Sure, that's one way to do it." She said it before thinking it through. Oooh. "Or the microwave kind is good. Look there's the bus."

What was she thinking? Or *not* thinking, as the case may be? Her engines were truly combustible around Beau, and another will-compromising position with Beau as the embers died down could push things too far too quickly.

"Now, look alive. Here's the bus. See you after school."

Sophie trudged back inside, took one look at her textbook, and cringed. She couldn't study today, not after what had happened last night.

Who had she become? And what must Beau think of her?

She wrapped a few presents, including the books she'd bought for everyone, but she was as wadded up inside as the wrapping paper she'd had to discard after making a mess of a gift-wrapping attempt.

I have to see him and gauge his reaction.

Then the perfect idea hit her. She'd head downtown, maybe to Mario's, and grab lunch for him.

Chapter 16

Beau

Beau stared at the blanks in the fillable form. They were a little blurry in his vision, but he'd been able to pound out a few sentences here and there, at least.

In his defense, this time he had something filling his mind, instead of just general mental paralysis. Today, at least, he was thinking about Sophie, her kiss, her reaction, and then Olympia's subsequent phone call.

"Beau, I've been thinking about you." Olympia had oozed seduction even over the phone. *"I know it's late, but every time I see you at work, you're all wound up."*

Beau hadn't been wound up last night, though. Sophie had loosened everything. Even his responses to Olympia.

"Don't you need to loosen up? I could help with that."

Yeah, Olympia probably could. Especially if Sophie actually did think of kissing Beau as a mistake. *"What do you have in mind?"* he'd asked.

They'd decided on dinner. Tonight. At Mario's.

"Well, Beau, my boy." Aunt Elaine stood at the door of his office. "I hear you're finally taking my advice."

"Oh?" He swung around in his desk chair to face her. "I pride myself on being willing to accept good advice. But what is it I'm doing?"

"You know. Dating again."

How had Aunt Elaine heard? "I mean, I've only really been out with her to the Hot Cocoa Festival." And the Waterfall Lights, if that counted, even though they never left the car. "Unless you count going with the kids to take cookies to our neighbor." Or a swim.

"One more date and you're in Sugaplum Falls's third-date kiss territory." Aunt Elaine gave an exaggerated wink that moved her cropped white hairline. "But forgive me for laughing at the picture of Olympia Barron out delivering cookies with children. Did she really do that?"

Olympia! Beau's office chair rolled backward a foot and crashed into the bookshelf behind him. He steadied his voice. "Olympia Barron?"

"She told me about your date tonight. Mario's, eh? Very good choice. Women swoon for their marinara sauce. If you've already been out twice, then tonight you should be getting some dessert." Aunt Elaine made kiss lips. She should not make kiss lips. "Am I right?"

"I mean, Olympia and I are having dinner together tonight." Was it a date? Probably, since she'd offered to *loosen him up* on it. "But it's a working dinner, for key players in the contract approval process. We're discussing the application." Probably. Maybe not. Why was his upper lip twitching?

"Then who was your date to the ... oh, never mind. I won't pry. I'll just say I'm thrilled to hear you're getting out again. *Especially* if it's with Olympia. The two of you could consolidate forces here at Tazewell, and, ahem, elsewhere. If you know what I mean."

Aunt Elaine gave a knowing chuckle and turned to go, but not without bumping into someone. "Excuse me. Oh! Are you the delivery girl from Mario's? Already? Why, Beau"—Elaine turned around—"you dog. In the daytime? Couldn't wait for tonight to ply Olympia with the marinara and get her into a third-date mood even if it's your first date, eh? Good for you." She gave one of those fast golf claps and then cackled her way down the hall.

"It's a company dinner tonight," he hollered after Elaine, while hustling to the door to see what was going on with a food delivery. Probably for another staffer.

Instead, he saw was a swish of unmistakable straight blonde hair climbing back onto the elevator before the doors closed. Sophie! Oh, no.

Beau made a dash for the elevator and slapped the down-button, but he was too late. He charged toward the stairs, racing down the flights two steps at a time, until he reached the ground floor, just as Sophie stepped through the automatic sliding doors toward the front parking area. But he was too late, and he nearly bumped into a woman pulling a massive cartload of beautiful poinsettias.

"Is the executive area on the fourth floor?" she asked. "I've got the town contract for placing them in all the businesses."

"Yeah. Up the elevator over there." Beau nodded, but he raced for the glass exit doors. Outside, Sophie's car was nowhere to be seen.

He shot her a text. *Sophie, were you here? I couldn't catch you, if you were. Inspiration finally hit for my project. I'll be working through the evening, and then there's a business/company dinner. Can you take care of the kids?*

Monosyllabic text response came: *Yep.*

No other explanation. But Beau couldn't worry about that. Somehow, seeing the swish of Sophie's long hair while he was in the Tazewell building had jarred something loose in him—suddenly unblocked the highways in his brain, or whatever, and suddenly Beau was typing up the best persuasive prose he'd ever concocted.

He was a contract application genius.

What was more, the knot in his neck didn't hurt today. It hadn't hurt since last night, as a matter of fact. *Was that due to Sophie's kiss, or to the phone call from Olympia afterward, offering to help him loosen up?* No telling for sure, but as of the past twenty-four hours, the Real Beau was back in business. He almost wished he could put one of those white checkmarks in a blue circle floating over his head—to show he was officially himself again.

Two hours of concentrated effort followed. He made some progress! The specs of the software's foliage-penetrating radar capabilities were now inputted in exact detail, and triple-checked. Finally. The main roadblock to his completion was behind him. The rest should be smooth sailing.

Just before the seven o'clock reservations, Beau typed the final sentence in the final box of fillable forms. He sent the duplicate to Olympia first, and then to everyone on staff, and asked for them to approve it. Much sooner than he expected, responses flowed in, so Beau pressed the *SUBMIT* button.

The application for the nine-figure government contract was in. As soon as December twenty-fourth at five o'clock p.m. Eastern Time, Beau, Aunt Elaine, Olympia Barron, and the rest of Tazewell Solutions staff and stockholders could learn their fate, and whether they were going to experience the best or the worst Christmas morning of their lives.

Fifteen minutes later, Beau arrived at dinner. Soft violins played Christmas music, while oregano and garlic wafted through the air of Mario's Italian restaurant.

Beau clinked his goblet against Olympia's. "To hitting *send.*"

"To hitting *send,*" she echoed. "And to your brilliantly persuasive prose in that application." She pressed the glass to her full lips and watched him over the top rim. Her gaze was accompanied by a weight Beau felt in his chest.

"You read it?"

"Of course." She blinked. Her eyelashes were extra thick. Fluffy, almost. "And I must say, it was worlds better than your earlier drafts. The clear, concise explanation you gave about the technology we've developed at Tazewell, plus the various applications, both military and for search and rescue? The work of genius. Do tell what inspired you. If it's a woman's encouragement, I won't mind hearing that, either."

In fact, it had been a woman's encouragement, but—maybe not in the way Olympia Barron would like to hear. "I guess my mental kinks got worked out." Right about the same time Sophie's hands on his skin and lips on his own had worked out his physical kinks.

Beneath the table, a fluttering disturbed Beau's pant leg. Were those ... toes? Olympia's toes slid up Beau's shin. His calf muscle seized, keeping his leg in place.

She dipped her eyes. "We really do make a powerful team, Beau. You have to admit, when we win this government contract, Tazewell is going to shoot into the stratosphere. We're going to do it. Together."

Beau swallowed, but his mouth had dried. "Everyone on the team contributed." He glanced toward the door of Mario's Italian. "Who else was planning on coming tonight? I thought ..." He thought she'd said to expect a few key players, as a dinner celebration. "Key players, right?"

A slow, knowing smile spread over her wide mouth. "Tonight it's about the two key players in this achievement."

Beau took a breadstick from the basket and broke it in half, and then each of those in half again. "We don't have the contract award yet."

"Oh, but we will." She traced a light fingertip over the back of Beau's hand. "Thanks to you."

Beau inhaled sharply. "Thanks for your confidence."

"I won't pretend. You did have me concerned for a while. You had a rough year leading up to this, but you pulled through." Her fingers wrapped around the side of his hand. "That New Year's Eve company dinner at Frosty Ridge is going to be a celebration of your glory."

"We don't have the contract yet." They'd just done everything they could do, and now it was time to cross fingers, wait, and pray their guts out.

Beau would be announcing huge bonuses for everyone who contributed, if it happened. Until then, however, Beau was in a worse situation: figuring out how to even make payroll for the company employees. He'd better start putting out clarion calls for a short-term loan to get them through the next payday.

If he couldn't make payroll right before Christmas, he'd be letting Pops down, even though they were on the brink of something huge. The last thing Beau could live with would be the tanking of the business Pops had entrusted to him.

"Speaking of that New Year's Eve dinner." Olympia's toes trailed gently up his shin and down again. "I ran into Jordan McNair, owner of the resort. He mentioned you have a question mark beside your *plus one* RSVP."

"McNair offered that information?" Beau should fire him.

"Well, more or less." Olympia lifted and dropped one of her mostly bare shoulders. She'd taken off her work blazer a moment ago and only wore a thin-strapped red camisole beneath.

Sophie looked good in red, too, like when they'd decorated the tree together, and Beau had nearly kissed her then. If he'd had any idea of how incredible a kiss with Sophie could be, he would have dragged her out of earshot of the kids and locked a door and become Captain Firestarter himself.

Sophie was a sneak attack. At first glance, she looked like the kid next door, but when the moment struck, she came out far sexier than Tracey, and even knocked Olympia into a distant second place slot.

"Jordan may or may not have left his list on my desk for a moment unattended." Olympia stirred her penne pasta with the tines of her fork. "I know how to take advantage of an opportunity."

118

Beau side-eyed her. At least Beau wouldn't have to fire Jordan. "I have someone in mind I'd like as my plus one." Unfortunately, she only had plans to stay in Sugarplum Falls until Christmas, not beyond.

"Why haven't you asked her yet?" Olympia held her fork aloft, suspending it in front of her full, parted lips. "She will probably say yes."

"Maybe." Beau couldn't guarantee it. She did accept phone calls at inopportune moments from men with designated love-song ring tones on her phone, right when Beau was feeling so close to her, and …

Wait a second. Olympia was talking about herself. Being out of the dating world for a decade and a half, he wasn't really up on all the social cues. "I'm still weighing my options. Jordan and I talked about it, and he's cool with letting me confirm at the last minute."

"No sense waiting until the eleventh hour, Beau." Olympia blinked her eyes slowly. "I know you and Tracey went through some rough times, but you're coming through that, and there's someone ready and available to repair all those hurts and fill all those empty places."

Beau pinched the stem of his goblet between his fingers, twisting it back and forth. "Actually, I'm starting to heal already."

Except for the fact that Sophie had rushed away from him last night, and again today when he'd seen her at Tazewell. And except for the fact that she'd looked so disturbed by the fact he'd taken advantage of her admitted weakness in the firelight.

Did she really think of their kiss as a mistake?

Olympia's toes unmistakably slipped along his ankle. Right across from him sat a woman who definitely wouldn't consider a physical escalation with Beau a mistake. In fact, she was practically begging him for it.

Olympia and I make sense. Aunt Elaine had been lobbying for it. Suddenly, Olympia seemed to be open as well. If he shut this door, based on one kiss with his ex-wife's little sister, would he be making yet another huge error in judgment when it came to women?

I've been burned by a Hawkins girl before. Not that Tracey and Sophie are alike, but still.

"To the future." Olympia held her goblet up for Beau to add his salute.

She caused not only his glass to rise, but also his blood, with the way she was staring. She wouldn't require three dates for him to kiss her. She sipped from her glass, but then, she sobered. "Beau, I need to ask you something. Something personal."

Uh-oh. They hadn't spoken about personal things up to now. Flirtation here and there, but nothing real. "Shoot."

"What do you want? I mean, what do you *really* want?"

"Besides the contract from the government and to be able to see Tazewell Solutions succeed?"

"Besides that."

The answer was easier than any other he could give, but was he ready to share it with Olympia? Moreover, was Olympia Barron ready to hear his answer? *If not, then she'll drop me quickly.* "Bluntly, I want an intact, nuclear family. I want my kids to have a mother." Not just a mother figure. "My kids are everything to me, even more than the company. They're incredible, and they've been stalwarts through this year's mayhem."

"Adele and Mac." She said their names softly. "They're very cute. Adele favors her mother."

And has Sophie's laugh. "She does." But Beau hadn't completed his want-list. "Besides the family being for them, though, I want a good marriage to ground me. One where I can give and receive."

Slowly, Olympia set down her goblet. She leaned back in her chair and gave him a hard stare. "So, not a fling, or a temporary girlfriend, or arm candy for all your meetings with government officials."

"Nothing like that." At all. Something real. Something permanent.

"Beau, you do astound me. In good ways, all good." She gave him a slow smile. "I knew Tracey—probably better than you would guess."

"Really? Did you spend time with her?"

"Yes." Olympia didn't elaborate, but it didn't take much time with Tracey to sound her depths. Or the lack of them. "You're looking for that ideal."

Exactly. Well, Tracey hadn't been ideal, but if Olympia knew her well, she caught the drift. "I mean, we're all approximating the ideal, no matter what. But I'd like a close version." Despite his initial complete failure in the marriage department, he could try again, right? Real Beau believed in success.

Olympia continued her close examination of him. "Could you achieve that ideal with any of the women you've hired as nannies?"

Beau spluttered, choking on his water. "Gosh, no." Giselle, Gemma, or Gigi? His upper lip curled. "Never. Not one of them comes close to being an option."

Olympia's mouth went into a flat line, and she crossed her arms over her chest, blinking as if computing his response. Then, a slow smile spread over her face and she relaxed back into her feline stance. "Beau Cabot, please know that I would do almost anything in the world to make you happy."

She would? Despite the ice water he'd just sipped—and sprayed—heat coursed across Beau's cells. "Olympia, I—"

She looked at her nails, and pulled one of her sly smiles. "Give me a few days to put something together."

Beau's mouth took a quick trip to the desert. "What do you have in mind?"

"The best Christmas surprise you'll ever get. It'll take some maneuvering, but I'll make your wishes come true." She leaned forward, and in the most tantalizing voice said, "By Christmas, you'll have both your government contract deal sealed, as well as the needs of your heart all sorted out. I'm a highly capable woman. Trust me."

Chapter 17

Sophie

"You've got this, you've got this, sweetie." Sophie crossed her fingers and held her breath as Adele, one of the two finalists, listened to the word a second time on the stage of the auditorium at the Sweetwater Theater in downtown Sugarplum Falls. Every family of every contestant had turned out in force to listen to the spellers and cheer for the eventual champion.

"Can you use it in a sentence, please?" Adele asked into the microphone. The judges complied. Adele stared blankly at her feet.

Sophie tensed in her theater seat. *Please let her spell it right.* They were down to the bitter end here, the final two spellers, and the last kid had misspelled the word *ignorant,* after which Adele had correctly spelled it. If she got this word right, she was the town speller. If not, she was thrown back into the competition.

Defusing bombs couldn't be more intense than this. Sophie would have to ask Beau if he'd ever had to do that during his career in the Air Force. *If he ever speaks to me personally again.* Ever since their kiss, he'd been distant. Maybe Sophie shouldn't have run off when she heard that older, cackling woman say those things about dating Olympia Barron when Sophie brought him lunch yesterday. Yes, Sophie had inferred the worst. Of course she had! And she'd dropped the meal and dashed to the parking lot to cry it out.

Then, of course, Beau had ended up explaining that away in his text. Not that Sophie had been emotionally up to replying much. Hearing about him even fictionally dating another woman the day after he'd kissed Sophie jarred her enough that she'd needed cool-down time.

Then, he'd worked late on Friday. Or, he'd gone out for dinner, and then acted like Sophie didn't exist when he got home or when he left for work this morning.

Kissing him was the worst mistake. He wishes I didn't exist. He wants me gone—just like I should have kept in the forefront of my mind all along.

Beside Sophie, Beau sat ramrod straight. Was he even breathing? Maybe not, but his lips were moving, as if in silent prayer.

Sophie shot one heavenward on Adele's behalf, too.

"Consummate. C-o-n-s-u-m-m-a-t-e. Consummate."

Of all words! What was with this spelling bee committee and words like *abstinence* and *consummate?* But she'd done it! The judge announced, "That is correct." The crowd surged to their feet, clapping for Adele, who smiled so broadly her face might crack, and little tears formed at the sides of her eyes.

Tracey was a fool for missing this moment, this child, this amazing young woman.

"Way to go, my precious!" Beau gathered Adele in his arms.

Mac thrust the grocery store bouquet of roses he'd brought along for Adele, win or lose. "Good job. You won. Now they're going to expect me to win next time." He sounded glum.

Adele threw her arms around Sophie's waist. "I couldn't have done it if you hadn't quizzed me, Aunt Sophie. Did you hear? I got the word *giraffe*. I would have done two Rs and one F if you hadn't picked that one for me to practice."

Sophie hugged her back. "You're amazing, you know that?"

Mac sighed heavily. "I just wish Mom could've seen it."

Sophie and Beau exchanged a glance. The look in his eyes said, *You and me both, kid.*

Did he miss Tracey? Or did he miss the idea of family more? It was definitely a hankering for the past. *A past utopia that probably didn't exist, if Tracey was involved.* Still, if only Sophie could give that to them in Tracey's stead. A family, a real family.

I could. If Beau wanted me to. But since he didn't, and since her kissing him was a mistake, it was better if she planned on leaving Sugarplum Falls by Christmas, to take her boards examination, and then to stay put in Darlington. Where she and Beau would be well outside of each other's Inappropriate Temptation Zones.

A large woman waddled up to them. "Oh, let me be one of the first to congratulate you." She kind of bowed. "I haven't met you," she said to Sophie. "I'm Shelby Forger, on the Sugarplum Falls town council. And I must say what a beautiful couple you are, as parents of such a brilliant daughter. How proud you must be. And, my, how Adele favors her pretty young mother." She beamed at Sophie, fluffed Adele's ringlets, and then beamed again before leaving.

Again? Someone assumed she and Beau were together? Of course they did. They went everywhere together, did everything as a family. She and Beau even had the sparks going of a real family—sometimes. They were more or less the nuclear family Sophie had always dreamed of creating of her own— with a few glaring differences. *One being we can't get a word in about what happened the other night in front of the fire.* They really did need to discuss that kiss, and what it meant going forward.

Or if it didn't mean anything.

"What do you say we go to The Orchard to celebrate?" Beau side-hugged Adele. "They have a playground there. I'll push you both on the swings."

Oh, dear. Even though Sophie was riddled with misgivings about how Beau felt about her, when he was being the world's best dad, there was no question how she felt about him. He cut down all her doubts with his fatherhood perfections.

I hope I can find someone as great as Beau someday. For my own children.

Could that be Dr. Matt Vaughn?

Man, her emotions and thoughts were a wildly broad pendulum today. *Get it together! He doesn't want you.*

Beau parked the SUV at Kingston Orchard. "Let's get outside, get on those swings while we can—before the sun abandons us again at sunset."

"It's so pretty," Sophie said. There was a clearing in front of a whole hillside covered with similarly shaped fruit trees. Their branches were bare this time of year, but every one of them was covered in lights. Hundreds, thousands of trees, and millions of lights. It was like a brilliant firefly display for acres and acres. "I didn't know the town had such a great place for kids to play."

"I forget you haven't spent much time in Sugarplum Falls. It definitely has some great places. The Orchard has a nice walking trail through it, and they turn on the lights like this in the evening, and everyone comes to walk. There's a place to buy fruit pies and jams up the way. My kids, however, are all about the playground."

"We love the playground!" Adele danced toward the playground.

"Yeah, we love it." Mac punched the air in a karate move. "I love the swings most."

The kids ran off. When Sophie turned back to Beau to confirm, he sat slack-jawed.

"What's wrong?" Alarm rattled her chest. "Is everything okay?"

"More than." Beau's eyes were wide. "Did you hear that? Mac just said swings—without the lisp."

"Yeah." Of course he did. While Beau had spent last night at work—or at dinner with Catwoman—Sophie had worked with Mac until the *S* happened correctly every time. "He finally got it last night."

"You did it, Sophie." Beau's eyes softened. "I'm just … floored. Wow."

"He worked hard. It was one of those big moments, you know? And it felt great, not just to him but to me. It's the reason I want to be a speech therapist."

"You're so good with kids." One side of his mouth rose. "I'd hate to—"

"Daddy! I'm upside down!" Adele interrupted his words, and he didn't finish.

Hate to what? Hate to lose her? Hate to let Mac and Adele lose Sophie's guidance? Hate to let Olympia Barron and her panther-like walk interfere with his and Sophie's future together—forever?

He turned back to her. "Adele is so much more confident than she was all summer." He started strolling the perimeter, and Sophie fell into step beside him.

"She was pretty amazing on the stage."

"I'm seeing her stand taller."

Adele wasn't the only one. Beau's posture was different today, too. He stood taller, his shoulders squarer, his jaw firmer. He looked … like *Beau*. The Beau Cabot Sophie had fallen in puppy-love with as a girl.

Except not. Because this Beau had more depth, strength, and experience. No, this was the Beau she'd fallen head over heels for as a woman.

They walked alongside each other, dodging the snowier places on the paved trail. Having him at her side felt so comforting, like he would protect her from … whatever. Wolves? Bears? Monsters? None of those were likely to appear in Sugarplum Falls, but still. He was good to walk beside.

"Oh, I should tell you. We completed that huge project for work. Just made the deadline, actually. Last night."

"The application for the government contract?" They kept to the path that circled the playground area, keeping an eye on Adele and Mac.

"You remember. Yeah."

"That's fantastic, Beau." Of course she remembered. It was an enormous deal—and the future of his stepdad's business rode on it. Should she high-five him? Hug him? "That's enormous." The culmination of years of effort, from what Sophie understood. "Oh, right. That's why you texted to say you were working late. How did you celebrate? Pizza for everyone, right?"

Beau kicked a snowdrift as they passed one. "There was Italian food at the staff celebration, for sure."

He was being weirdly evasive. Maybe she was prying. She'd drop it, but—oh. Suddenly, she put the two incidents together. The dinner mentioned by the lady with the cackle, the one with Olympia Barron, had been the celebration dinner. And he'd definitely come home late and *without* checking in with Sophie afterward other than to dash past her in the living room with a spring in his step.

And today he was walking on sunshine, despite the subzero temperatures.

Sophie's heart dropped halfway to her knees.

"Beau! I never see you here on Sunday afternoons."

At that voice, and the sight of the speaker, Sophie's heart dropped from her knees straight onto the icy sidewalk. Up slithered none other than the woman who'd captured Beau's heart.

Olympia leaned in and gave Beau one of those European two-cheek kisses hello. "What a nice surprise." The tall, seductive figure of Olympia Barron loomed over Sophie, and Sophie was forced to take a defensive step

126

back. "I mean, I guess I did mention last night over dinner we come here every Sunday afternoon for a stroll through the trees, so you knew I like it here." She petted the little dog in her arms.

"Cute dog." Sophie didn't reach for it.

"Thanks. Luvvums and I love the park, don't we?" She baby-talked the dog, suddenly looking and sounding—unexpectedly—almost maternal. "That penne pasta last night was delectable. Thank you for dinner, Beau. It was great to finally sit down, just the two of us, and rejoice over our shared victory."

Suspicions confirmed. Just the two of them. Dinner. And Beau had come back to Turtledove Place practically skipping and doing the Macarena. Sophie's eyes riveted on the little happy dog so that she wouldn't shoot lasers out of them into Olympia's brain and scramble it.

Or at Beau, for that matter.

In her peripheral vision, however, Beau shifted his weight. Good. He should be squirming. He'd lied about dinner with Olympia. He'd said it was a celebration for his staff.

Staff of two. Humph.

But, please. Beau didn't belong to Sophie! Even if she'd kissed him in the misguided mellow glow of firelight. Nor could she have any claim on him. In fact, every time they'd gotten closer, she'd bolted. Certainly, she'd sent mixed messages. No wonder he was looking elsewhere for what Sophie shouldn't give him.

Yet. *I just need to talk to Matt. In person. Like we agreed on the phone the other night.* After the kiss.

She could date everything by acronym now: BKB, Before Kissing Beau, and AKB: After Kissing Beau.

Her stomach churned again, sounding like a cement mixer. Sophie must tell Beau what were her real feelings for him.

And to definitely show him, too.

Unless Olympia beat Sophie to the punch.

Olympia's little doggie yapped, and the puppy-mama soothed it before turning her imperious gaze back on Sophie. "Sophie, dear, how long are you planning on staying?"

"Until Christmas."

"She has a test to take down in Darlington," Beau added.

"Daddy! Push me on the swing!" Mac's legs dangled below the swing, limp, his whole body a mass of dejection, while beside him Adele soared.

"I'm going high already, Daddy. You don't have to push me." She stuck out her tongue at Mac, who started to moan-cry.

"Sorry. Duty calls. I'd better go and just ..." Beau jogged toward the kids.

"Oh, honey. You're still a co-ed. Isn't that sweet? I knew you were young, but I hadn't imagined ..." She laughed behind her hand. "It's really time Beau grew up a little."

With no Beau to protect or defend her, Sophie was on her own against this enemy—whose superior firepower was obvious. "I wouldn't say *co-ed*," she muttered. Weak!

As if she hadn't heard Sophie, Olympia went on. "The great dad act is irresistible, isn't it?" Her cat-eyed gaze followed Beau.

It's not an act. "He's been a brick lately, considering everything."

"Exactly. It's good of you to try and stand in for your sister, since she, um ..."

Nobody needed to tell Sophie about Tracey's faults. "Yeah, my sister and I never really saw eye to eye."

"Maybe not, but considering how similar you are in appearance to her, if by some accident Beau acts like he's attracted to you, I'm sure you've already chalked that up to ten-plus years of marriage to your twin."

Thank you? Where was the passably civil woman Sophie had met at the Hot Cocoa Festival? It must have been an act for Beau's benefit.

Olympia sighed and petted her dog. "I really don't know how Beau can stand to have you around as a reminder all the time. Have you given any thought to his feelings at all?"

Lots. All her thoughts, actually. "What are you getting at?"

"Beau Cabot is a broken man." Olympia's dog yapped, as if for an exclamation point. "He needs a wife—a real wife—to heal his wounds."

That could be Sophie. No two sisters could ever be more different. Sophie would be exactly the opposite of Tracey. "Did you have someone in mind, Olympia?" Herself, most likely. Sophie kept her tone and her gaze steady—on the dog.

"Naturally, I do. In fact, while we were at dinner last night, Beau and I solidified plans for New Year's Eve up at the Frosty Ridge Lodge. As you probably know, Sugarplum Falls is most famous for two things, third-date kisses and New Year's Eve proposals."

Sophie's mouth went dry. "Oh, really?" Even though Sophie shouldn't want to go claws-out, she did have to curl her fingers into her palms as a precaution. "That's nice." Ice coated her words.

Sophie shouldn't care about this, shouldn't drink the poison. By New Year's Eve, as far as Beau knew, she'd be long gone—back to Darlington, back to Dr. Matt and her life that she had originally planned, until now. Until the swim and the fire and the kissing.

"What Beau needs is a wife. A partner. His equal. Someone his match intellectually. To live in his house and be everything a wife should be."

"Naturally." *Do not grind your teeth audibly, or she'll hear you. Don't let her get to you.* "And someone to raise his children." And sit with him beside the fire at night and talk about the kids' needs. *And kiss his loneliness away.* "Someone who will nurture his kids, love them, and put them first."

For a split-second, Olympia recoiled. Then she composed herself. "Beau, as a husband, should be put first. I know just the woman to do that."

"Good luck with your quest." Or hunting party, going in for the kill, or whatever. *Because I highly doubt you're what Beau is looking for.* "And for the record, you're right. He was broken. But he's a much stronger man than you give him credit for, and he's healing faster every day."

Olympia was unfazed. "I knew from the second I laid eyes on you that you wanted him. It's sick, you know? He's your brother."

"It just means I love his kids like they belong to me, because they do."

"The kids." Olympia's scoff scratched the dry winter air. "He will choose a wife. And he will choose with his passions, not his compassion. It's the only way for a man to be truly satisfied. Trust me. I know enough about men to know this."

Maybe that was true. But Beau definitely had exhibited passion toward Sophie the other night.

But that was before all the awkwardness, and before the insertion of Olympia Barron and her tête-á-tête dinner parties and her possessiveness on full display. And now ... he was taking this serpent-like woman with too much eye makeup to dinner and asking her out to New Year's Eve? Everyone knew what happened at midnight on New Year's Eve—but it seemed like in Sugarplum Falls, even more happened.

Sophie's upper lip curled involuntarily. No! Beau could not kiss Olympia Barron. If there was one woman in Sophie's acquaintance worse than Tracey, it was this huntress.

And Beau clearly wanted her. *More than he wants me.*

Olympia looked at the long, blood-red fingernails on her free hand. "I heard him saying just last night that he wishes his family were intact again." She sighed as if she had a secret. Or as if she had a lie. It was hard to tell which with this woman. "He's so glad he's found someone who can make that happen for him very soon." She dipped her chin and closed her eyes, as if humbly accepting her crown as Beau's queen.

"Really. He said that. Implying you as that person." Her voice was flat, without question inflections.

Olympia smiled wanly. "Merry Christmas, Little Tracey Wannabe." She slithered away up the path into the trees. If only Sophie had had a snake hook and could lift her up and drop her in the snake pit where she belonged, with the other boa constrictors.

Sophie felt her neck, to see if there were any residual strangle marks.

I will not let her get to me. I will not let her get to me.

But it was too late. Beau's words from earlier echoed back.

I would hate ... he'd begun. *He'd hate to keep me from that life as a speech therapist, when I'm so good with kids. He would hate to mess up his relationship with that temptress. He'd hate to let me get in the way.* He wanted Sophie gone.

A full-force Mac pummeled into Sophie's legs. "Guess what I asked Santa for in my letter we had to write at school?" Every *S* came out perfectly.

"What, honey?"

"For a mommy." He pointed at Olympia. "That one has a puppy already. She'd be perfect."

Ka-powie. Sophie nearly doubled over. Mac was the last person Sophie expected to side with Olympia. Strike two. Ouch.

"Mac." Adele marched toward them, hands on her hips in full Scold Mac mode. "I heard you. And it's not nice. Besides, we already have someone perfect for us. No puppy required." She beamed up at Sophie. "Our mommy. Tracey Hawkins Cabot."

Sophie's insides sliced, as if she'd eaten broken glass. Three strikes, and she was out. Out of the inning, the game, and the whole ballpark.

It turned out no one wanted her at Turtledove Place after all.

Chapter 18

Beau

Beau was dying to get Sophie alone to have a serious conversation. It'd been days since their steamy kissing session in front of the fireplace—followed by her terrified reaction. He had to get to the bottom of that, so that he'd know what to do next.

I want her. But if she doesn't want me, the last thing I'm going to do is clip her wings.

Of all people in the world, Sophie deserved to fly. She'd always loved planes and flight and—and it was what had drawn him to her in the first place. And, in an accidental way, to Tracey. If he hadn't noticed Sophie as a brilliant young girl, with all that light coming from her, he might not have ever spotted Tracey or taken notice of her that day.

However, since they returned from the park in the evening, Sophie had been more than distant. She'd been positively curt with him. Finally, the kids went to bed, and Beau was just leaning into the grate to set the logs and kindling, when Sophie walked down the stairs.

"I told the kids good night—and goodbye. I'll be leaving in the morning."

Beau dropped his match. "What?" He looked up at her. "Weren't you staying until Christmas?"

"It's almost Christmas." Her voice was flat, and she wouldn't make eye contact with him. "School is out. Your project has been submitted. The spelling bee is done, Mac can pronounce the letter *S*, and you've given them a good Christmas. No question. So, yeah. I'm probably not needed anymore."

His eardrums were like trampolines, her words landing and bouncing right off again. "Sophie—"

"It turns out I can take my boards as soon as I like, and there's someone I promised to spend time with."

"Matt." That was the name Beau had heard Sophie use over the phone a few times. "Is he someone important to you?" He stood and left the fire unlit, walking toward her, but she took a step backward from him.

"He's my boss." She looked at her shoes. "Yeah, he's important. He'd like us to be more important to each other."

"He's why you're leaving?" It didn't make sense. Just a few days ago, Sophie had been as into Beau as he'd been into Sophie, whether or not she blamed the fire's glow. Beau knew chemistry, and it had been off the charts. Yes, Olympia still asserted herself now and then, invading his thoughts, but Sophie's kiss was ... whoa. No question, he wanted it again. He wanted her. "It feels kind of sudden. The kids were expecting you through Christmas."

"Oh, the kids will be just fine without me. I have no doubt." Sophie straightened her spine and squared her shoulders. "But I do have one question for you. Did you tell Olympia that you would never consider creating a family with someone who was in your home to help you with Mac and Adele?"

"Of course I did." Duh. No nannies for Beau. Ever. "I do have standards."

Sophie's ice-blue gaze grew a little watery, and she sniffed once. "Okay. Well, I know I said I was leaving in the morning, but since I'm packed, and there may be snow overnight, I think I'll head back to my apartment tonight. And in case there's a storm coming, I want to beat the weather system, since we know about avalanche danger."

Sophie was talking a mile a minute, and Beau was still reeling from the fact she was leaving immediately.

"But ... what about Christmas?" he asked again, dumbly.

"I've been talking with Matt, actually"—Sophie turned away and headed for the staircase—"and I'm seriously considering taking his offer."

"Job offer?" Beau trailed after her, taking two stairs at a time to keep up.

"Uh—uh-huh." She paused on the first landing. "Offers, I should say. I'm thinking of taking all of them." She climbed again.

Wait—was this Matt dude offering more than a job? Beau's soul clunked. She'd said Matt was her boss but would like them to be more to each other. "Sophie, but what about Christmas?" he asked again, as if the last time he'd said it he'd spoken a foreign language that she hadn't understood.

On the second landing she stopped and turned around. In a voice firmer than he'd ever heard her use, even with the kids, she answered him. "Look, Beau. For the past month, you have created a whole feast of holiday traditions for you and the kids. From snowmen to cookie-delivery, from the cocoa festival to the Waterfall Lights. Decorating the tree, all of it." She didn't mention the swimming. "What I'm saying is you're set. You've done all of this as a family, and I've been the fly in the ointment too long already."

What in the world was she talking about? "That's just ... inaccurate." Where was she getting this idea? "Who told you something like that?" If it was Olympia, Beau would have some serious words with the woman. *It has to be Olympia.*

Brushing off her trousers, as if dusting all of them off her soul, she said, "The children."

Chapter 19

Sophie

Crying and driving was worse than texting and driving, especially during snowstorms. Sophie had to pull over to the side of the road three times before leaving Sugarplum Falls proper and heading over the canyon. Then, she'd stopped twice in the canyon to blow her nose and dab her tears.

Finally at her apartment complex, she looked up and saw the wilted little paper chain hanging from the railing of the balcony outside her bedroom. Rain must have ruined it. Or Sophie's tears had existentially traveled to Darlington to mush the construction paper in some symbolism of her destroyed hopes of being a permanent part of Mac's and Adele's lives.

She lugged her suitcase up the staircase and went inside the apartment.

"Vronky?" she asked, peeking into her roommate's bedroom. "Are you awake?" Sophie's voice trembled, on the verge of avalanching into another donkey-cry.

"Sophie? What are you doing here? I thought you were in Sugarplum Falls until Christmas."

Every reason crowded her throat, but the one that spilled out was, "I told him I was leaving, and he didn't beg me to stay." Worse, the kids didn't want her. But if she said that aloud, she'd never stop crying as long as she lived.

Vronky gathered Sophie into her arms, and she cried on the couch in the light of the Christmas tree until she was practically dehydrated.

"You don't have to talk about details. Just cry it out." Vronky brought them each a glass of apple juice. "Matt dropped by earlier. Woke me up, actually."

Matt? "He did?" At least he hadn't forgotten her, hadn't shoved her away as unwanted. "What time? Did he say anything?"

"About a half hour before you came home. He looked nervous. Did you tell him you were coming—and not tell me?"

In a crying-induced haze, she had indeed texted him. "I probably shouldn't have."

"Well, he did have a gleam in his eye."

The gleam. Oh. That could be good or bad. "Did he say anything?"

"Just to have you call him as soon as you get here, but I didn't want to bring it up, since you were in full-on Beau-mourning mode."

Ugh. She was such a mess. She'd lost all of it, everything she'd almost let herself dream could belong to her. "I'm mourning the kids, too."

"Uh-huh." Vronky obviously knew the scales tipped toward Beau, as far as the crying went. "If he's really out of your life, dear, it's probably time to move on while the moving is good. Even though a really good door closed on you, Matt is your open window."

Chapter 20

Beau

On Christmas Eve morning, Beau sat in a stupor without Sophie to bring order to their lives. "Can't we open *any* presents tonight, Daddy?" Mac and Adele had been bugging Beau about gifts all afternoon. With no school, and no Sophie to care for them, Beau had been at Turtledove Place all day—trying and failing to work from his home office, succeeding only in watching the clock tick toward five o'clock.

The government contract award announcement could come today at five. Five o'clock daily. The Department of Defense announced contract awards on their website—for any contract over seven million dollars. Tazewell Solutions just had to be listed.

I'm also counting the minutes since Sophie left in the night.

"Please, Dad? One present?" The kids were lurking in his office again, begging to know what was under the tree. His phone chimed a text. Maybe it was Sophie! He lunged for it, but Adele had it in her hand already. "Daddy? Who is Olympia? And why is she promising us a good Christmas surprise?"

Before Beau could answer, Mac said, "She's the spider lady with the little dog."

Spider lady! Really? "Give me that." Beau took the phone from Adele. Sure enough, the text from Olympia promised a big Christmas morning surprise.

It's not just for you, Beau. It's what will make your children happiest. Get ready to rejoice.

Rejoice? Really? Was she actually thinking about how her gift was going to affect Adele and Mac? That was kind of out of Olympia's character, since mostly all she'd done was flirt outrageously with Beau. Of course, there was the moment when she shared her dog with Mac at the park. That had been all right. Olympia did have some skill with kids. Or, at least with dogs.

A second text came in. *Did you check the email? Government contract won't be announced today, or tomorrow, for the holiday. Let's check back on it Thursday. By then, I'm sure you'll be a very happy man.*

Blast it! No government announcement today! It made sense. He shouldn't have expected anything certain the week of Christmas. It was a good thing—a Christmas blessing, really—North Star Capital had come through with the temporary loan to float Tazewell Solutions through this week's payroll. In a moment of desperation, he'd offered North Star a percentage of his stock in Tazewell to secure the loan. But he'd been at wits' end. Not paying the employees on the week of Christmas was a new low Beau couldn't plumb.

Not having a company for them to work at would be far worse, though. He'd have to hold his breath a few more days. It was killing him.

Olympia's other topic had him squirming even more, however. A Christmas with Olympia was something he'd never envisioned.

"Not tonight, kids." He shut off his computer screen. No use staring into the void any longer. "Gifts are for Christmas morning."

"You sound like Aunt Sophie." Mac stomped his foot. "Where did she go, anyway? I miss her. Doesn't she love us anymore?"

From the way Beau heard it, they were the ones who'd told her to get lost. What could that possibly be about? "Sophie did send me a message. It's about your presents."

She'd texted him the night she left with a cryptic plea. *Please read the Christmas presents to the kids.* It had taken him a few minutes to process it, but when he checked under the tree, he found a pile of wrapped gifts for each of them, all obviously books.

There'd even been one for Beau. Which made him a jerk, since he'd been too busy worrying about Tazewell's future to get her anything.

Now, should he even bother?

Beau got the kids each a pizza pocket—not the home-made calzone kind, just the frozen ones he could put in the microwave.

Mac sighed. "Pizza pockets make me miss Aunt Sophie."

Adele pushed hers away. "The frozen ones really aren't that good." Beau couldn't argue with that. "Things tasted better when Sophie was here."

138

More than true. "I don't really have any answers for you about why she left, but I do know she needed to take her boards. She wants to be able to teach other kids besides Mac how to say the letter S."

"Aunt Sophie was good at helping me with that." Mac sighed again, this time a balloon with the air all being let out.

"And good at helping me study for the spelling bee." Adele picked at a crust. "She was good at everything."

Everything except maybe telling Beau what was on her mind. *I shouldn't have let her leave without getting to the bottom of her reaction to our kiss.* That had been his fatal error.

And now she was gone.

Beau put on a Christmas movie for himself and the kids, one he could enjoy, too—with no unicorn or rainbow Pegasus involved. But he couldn't seem to stay focused on whether or not the elf could make it back to the North Pole in time to help Santa. Instead, he leaned his elbow on the couch and put his head onto his hand.

All the while growing up, Mom had made the holidays wonderful—despite Dad's absence. There had been the rare years, though, when Dad showed up and ruined things with his terrible temper. Dad. Chuh. Beau would never understand Dad. Never, no matter how long he lived. Still, even during those times, Mom had smoothed it all over, made Christmas grand.

After Dad finally stopped coming around, Beau had vowed—solemnly—to create a family where the kids were safe and loved and cherished and where Christmastime love flowed in the air of their lives year-round.

Somehow, that reality had gotten away from him.

Now, here he sat, single dad, watching TV with the kids. This was the opposite of the Christmas fantasy he'd let himself weave over the past month with Sophie around. She'd promised tradition and joy—and she'd delivered. It wasn't just the best Christmas for the kids, it'd been the best holiday season of Beau's adult life. There'd been family time, laughter, meals, service, love.

And Sophie had made it all happen. What he'd wished for, the intact family, Sophie had delivered. She'd sprinkled Christmas joy and magic all over Turtledove Place, and then he'd let her get away without a fight.

The Real Beau wouldn't sit idly by and watch a great chance like having Sophie in his life and in the kids' lives get away from him.

But the problem was, without Sophie, Real Beau crawled back into his hibernation cave. He might not come out until spring. Or maybe ever.

She made me into the man I used to be, the man I'm supposed to be.

Without her, he was a shell of himself. He needed her, but she was gone.

The doorbell rang, and Adele ran to get it.

In came Aunt Elaine, arms laden. "I brought Christmas!" She filled his countertop with turkey dinner. "It's for tomorrow. We can reheat. I'd be back to help eat it, but a friend and I are heading out on Sugar Lake to do some ice fishing. Let's hope I don't fall through."

"A friend?" Beau asked.

"Oh, you know Lorne Behr. Owns the storage units with his sister."

"Sugarbear Storage?" Beau knew that guy. Widowed, really nice. Was this a date? "Sure. Nice guy. More teddy bear than grizzly bear, everyone says." Beau had only met him a couple of times at civic things. "Have you been seeing him lately?"

Aunt Elaine's eye sparkled. "I've been single so long I'd forgotten how good it feels to have someone in my life." She got a dreamy look for a moment, and then she lowered her chin and trained her gaze on Beau like it contained one of the guided missiles from Tazewell's R&D department. "You need a wife. Trust me."

Stabbed. Right in the heart. "I let one get away." Sophie was never coming back to him.

"Well, don't let her escape again. She's coming tomorrow, you know."

She was? "How do you know?" Beau's heart took flight.

"Olympia and I are in close contact."

Beau's heart impacted against cliffs. The Air Force had an acronym that would have described it perfectly: KCRLDF—*Killed in Crash Landing, Destroyed By Fire.*

"Olympia Barron." Beau couldn't. Not for himself, but also not for Adele and Mac. She wasn't a good fit for their family, which he couldn't see for the haze of grief this year had cast over his mind until now. She might get Beau's engines revving now and then, but … no. Even when she'd been trying to the other night at dinner with her toes against his ankles, Beau hadn't felt a fraction as much chemistry as he had with Sophie.

Plus, no way would Olympia traipse through snow to shovel the driveway for Mrs. Chan. Nor would she sit and admire the view of the lake and ask questions about Mom's life. Nor would she teach his kids to talk or spell or be kind.

Or make him wish he could light a fire in the grate every night.

Sophie. Sophie was the woman Beau needed. But the point was moot. Sophie didn't want him. She'd walked away from Turtledove Place, leaving him in a state where he couldn't think his way clear and was in a circling death spiral of logic.

"Merry Christmas again, Beau, kids." Aunt Elaine air-kissed them and left, still too much in her dating-Mr.-Behr haze to note Beau's full reaction to her suggestion about making Olympia Barron his wife. Thank goodness, or he would have had to argue, and he had no leg to stand on. Aunt Elaine would have made all the logical arguments, ending with the one that was most final: Sophie was gone.

Beau placed the turkey and side dishes in the refrigerator and stared at the containers filled with leftovers from meals Sophie had made. Soon those would be gone, too.

She doesn't want me. She wants that Matt guy. The kiss between them had been nothing but a replay of how Tracey had used him, right?

Maybe. Maybe not. It had felt too genuine, too real. Too bonding between them to be anything but sincere.

But yeah. She was gone. Before Christmas Eve, even.

Sophie. He couldn't have Sophie. He couldn't want Sophie.

But the fact remained, like Aunt Elaine had said, Beau did need someone. On his own, he'd been a wreck. Months now of wreckage.

Who else was there?

Who else was there who even would take him with all his faults besides Olympia?

Olympia was the path of least resistance.

141

In her text, she'd been solicitous of the kids' feelings. In fact, she'd verbally offered to sacrifice anything to make his wish for a traditional family happen.

Could it possibly be that Olympia wanted the traditional family dream for herself, too?

I guess the Cabots could make Olympia Barron's Christmas wish come true.

Chapter 21

Sophie

Darlington looked less bleak than when she'd left. In the stark morning sun, Sophie raised her hands against the glare, and the painted holiday scenes on some of the shops' windows became visible. It was kind of festive. Not Sugarplum Falls-level festive, but still. The town made an effort.

"Thanks for getting together with me." Matt had asked her to come at the stroke of noon, the second the clinic closed for Christmas Eve. "It's been a long time."

Sophie hugged him, and he took her by the hand. No snow was on the ground, just a few errant piles of leaves. No music played in the streets. Decidedly less festive, but still. She shouldn't complain. Some Christmas was better than none.

"How was Sugarplum Falls?" he asked as they passed a coffee shop with a bell-ringing Santa outside.

"Nice."

"Is there really a waterfall, or is it like one of those housing developments named after foxes and eagles that don't have any foxes or eagles?"

She described it for him, although she had to dial back raptures as she described the Waterfall Lights show on the frozen ice tower. "My niece declared it prettier than rainbow unicorn Pegasus wings."

"Kids." Matt shook his head. "Were you stuck babysitting all the time, or did the kids have school and give you a break?" For Matt, kids meant work.

"I missed them during the day, but we still had lots of fun in the evenings." Without giving away too much of her heartache, she gave Matt a thumbnail of her life there. She left out the more emotional bits, glossing over Beau's presence altogether.

"Sounds like one of those life-experiences you and I will look back on someday. *The month we were apart.*"

Sophie halted.

"What's the matter? Your scarf get caught on the fence?" A little iron fence made a box around one of the bare trees on the sidewalk. "No, you're all right." He gathered it up and handed her the tail of her scarf. "Is something wrong?"

Everything. Everything in the world. "I'm trying to figure out what you're thinking, Matt. I just … I wanted to process was all."

A smile crossed his face. "Oh, with the *someday we'll look back on these times* comment? Yeah, sorry about that. Probably getting ahead of myself."

Uh, yeah. They hadn't even really had the *we're dating* talk yet. Well, other than the fact they were meeting parents tomorrow. He'd even convinced her to take him to meet Mom and Dad, after going to see his folks.

Sophie winced. She shouldn't have agreed to that, but in her emotionally weakened state, she'd been too drained to disagree at the time. But now, she was at a crossroads. Two roads diverging in a yellow wood, and which one she chose would make all the difference.

She'd put so many decisions on hold until after passing her boards. And until after finding out Beau didn't want her in his life.

"No, you're not getting ahead of yourself, Matt. I'm ready to make some real decisions."

Matt lit up like that orchard in Sugarplum Falls she'd visited with Beau.

Why does everything have to make me think of that place? Of that man?

"I'm so glad to hear that!" Matt clapped his mittens together. "Let's head in here and talk."

"We are talking," Sophie said, but she allowed him to tug her into a bakery with seating. It wasn't nearly as cute as Sugarbabies Bakery in Sugarplum Falls. Nor did the proprietor have a big, toothy smile like Mrs. Toledo had.

"I mean really talk." Matt brought her a stale doughnut and a cup of cider. The cider paled by comparison to The Cider Press's beverage.

I'm almost as loyal to Sugarplum Falls now as I have been to Beau all these years. What a ridiculous way to be. Sophie would never live there again.

Matt didn't let her finish the doughnut before he launched. "It's the end of the year, as you know. Which means hiring time. The board of directors has bylaws and deadlines they need to meet."

"Yeah?" She tried dipping her doughnut in the cider to give it back a little moisture. It splashed over, burning the side of her hand.

"We've talked about that a few times in the past, I know."

A lot of times, actually. The deal was, Sophie would be hired as a full-time speech therapist at Darlington Speech Clinic, ready to begin January first.

"Did I mention? I took my boards last night." She couldn't sleep anyway, so she'd logged on and done them online. "They promised to send my scores by Friday. It's longer since Christmas Eve, Christmas, you know."

Matt nodded a lot, but the second she finished talking, he hopped in. "I'm glad you're ready to roll with this—as ready as I am." He reached for her hands across the table. "While you were out, we hired a new intern."

Sophie's mouth dried out. "I was replaced?"

"He's great with the kids. They are already calling him Uncle Billy."

"Uncle Billy?"

"Sure. Great guy. Lachlan Llewellyn asks for him by name."

I'm out—even though I'm the one who taught Lachlan his L sounds and made it possible for the kid to pronounce the name Billy.

So unfair!

He's not hiring me.

"Are you saying there's no job as a speech therapist at the Darlington clinic?"

Instead of his face falling, looking sad, the edges of Matt's mouth tilted upward. "I'm saying I need a partner."

Partner. "I just graduated, Matt. I don't have the money to buy into a practice."

He shook his head. "You're misunderstanding me." He pulled her hands across the table. "Tomorrow we're going to meet my parents. While we're there, I want to be able to tell them I have found my partner. For this life."

Whoa. Just hold up a minute. "Aren't we kind of skipping a few levels? Like exclusive dating, like escalating feelings for one another, like emotional commitment?" Like kissing until we can tell whether we have fiery chemistry? Now that Sophie had touched the flame, nothing else would do.

"All of that can come. And it will, in time."

A buzzing started in Sophie's ears. "Explain more fully?"

He did. It boiled down to what he'd said earlier: that at year's end, there was a hiring crunch. If Matt was dating Sophie, it would look strange, even unethical, if he hired her over that Uncle Billy person, who had stepped in when Sophie left without warning.

"I did kind of leave the clinic suddenly." But it was a family emergency! *Sort of. Really, I just wanted to see Beau.* And where had that gotten her? "I'm so sorry for the inconvenience it caused everyone on staff."

Matt forgave her, but there was more. "The truth is, I'm in a bit of a bad position with my investors." For inexplicable reasons, he needed a second board-certified clinician as a partner, but if he was dating Sophie and brought her in as partner, it would look bad; however, if they were engaged to be married—or better, married—the board had said they would overlook it. "They need an answer by Thursday."

"The day after Christmas?" Sophie gasped, nearly spilling her mediocre hot cider. "That soon?" She had to commit to both job and marriage instantly?

"Like I said at the outset of the conversation, it's the end of the year, and company bylaws state that staffing decisions must be in place by January one."

"What if I'm not board-certified by then?"

"You've taken the test. We both know you passed it."

Sophie didn't know that. Frankly, she didn't know much of anything at this moment. "You're moving really fast, Matt."

"Sophie." He leveled his softest gaze at her. "We've been dating for over half a year. Do you think I'd be dating *not* toward a fixed, defined purpose like a permanent relationship?"

No, actually. Matt was one of the most purpose-driven people she knew. "You were thinking marriage all along?"

"Of course I was. Weren't you?"

Had she been? Honestly, she had, because Dr. Matt Vaughn checked every box. He was kind, loyal, supportive, amicable, a good friend. "Are you proposing to me?"

He relaxed his grip and gave a breathy chuckle. "It's roundabout, isn't it? Not my usual style. I wanted you to have all the facts. I thought maybe if you knew all the facts, you'd consider it less abrupt, or realize that I wasn't pressing you for an immediate answer for no reason." Matt slipped from his chair and got down on one knee. He reached into his lab coat pocket. "I've been carrying this around for a while. Since Thanksgiving." He pulled out a green velvet box and opened it. "Sophie, will you be not just my partner in work, but in life?"

Chapter 22

Beau

Christmas morning meant presents and messes and squeals of delight—because there were children. Even without Sophie around. *Olympia's gift is coming soon, too.*

Beau pulled yet another pile of wadded wrapping paper out of Mac's way.

"Thanks, Daddy!" Mac spun the propeller on the toy plane. "I love flying! I'm going to grow up and be a helicopter pilot like Grandpa Cabot."

Beau's arm froze partway arched back to aim for the trash can, and he dropped the crumpled paper onto his lap. "How did you know that's what Grandpa Cabot did for a job?"

But Mac was too busy flying the helicopter around the room to answer.

"Did Mommy call?" Adele asked. "I thought … I thought she was coming back."

Mac crashed his chopper into a sofa cushion. "I don't want her back. She doesn't love us."

"Mac!" Beau spoke too loudly. "Of course she loves you—in her own way." With the faucet of love screwed down to *tiny trickle.* "She's your mother."

Mac harrumphed and crashed his toy again. "I thought I wanted Mommy to come back and be my mom all the time. I told her that a lot of times, but she didn't listen." He looked at his feet. "I told Sophie, too."

Beau dropped the package he'd picked up to hand to Adele. "You what?" It landed hard, probably making a bruise on his leg. He was losing his grip, literally.

"I'm sorry, Daddy." Adele looked at the floor. "When Mac said he wanted a mommy who already had a cute doggy for Christmas like that scary tall lady, I told everyone we already had one, and she was the only mom I wanted. I think Sophie was sad."

Beau closed his eyes, resisting the temptation to put his head into his hands. "Did this happen on the day that we went to The Orchard playground?"

Adele's eyes welled with tears, reddening instantly. Her lower lip trembled. "I made her go away."

It made sense, finally. What Sophie had said about the kids telling her she wasn't wanted. He stifled a groan, but Adele began to wail.

"I'm so sorry, Daddy."

Beau snatched her into his arms. "This isn't your fault, honey."

"Yes, it is. I acted like I didn't love Sophie that day. But I do."

"Aunt Sophie is like a real mommy." Mac spoke quietly, maybe for the first time in his life. "I miss her. She taught me to say *S* and she's going to help me with my *R*, but she left. Now she can't help me or be my friend or play with us in the snow to build a baby snowman to go with Mr. and Mrs. Snowman." Mac pronounced every *S* perfectly.

Beau set his jaw, keeping his face as sympathetic to the children as possible—but no amount of external pretense could prevent the million-crack shattering of his insides.

"Can we please at least open her presents, Daddy"—Adele wriggled out of his arms—"so it will seem like we didn't totally lose her?"

The kids might think so, but Beau was the one who'd lost her. Not them.

His instinct was to say no, out of self-preservation, but he relented under Adele's nine-year-old logic. Digging far beneath the Christmas tree where he'd more or less buried them, Adele found them and played elf, handing the gifts to each person.

"She got me lots of presents." Mac grinned, shaking one. "I think they're storybooks. She promised to read me stories. Aunt Sophie does the best voices."

They opened them one by one. "Should we read them right now?" The least Beau could do was to fulfill Sophie's wish and read the kids their presents, so he did. On the couch, in front of the empty grate where the fire should have been.

Adele liked her stories about a talking doll, and Mac loved the one about

149

the tractor the most, and then they went back over to the tree.

"Look, Daddy. The last one is for you." Adele excavated beneath the branches and brought out a heavy package.

On the gift tag, it read *Beau*. Plus, it was decorated with a little stylized helicopter—a Huey, hand-drawn.

The Huey. Dad's chopper. He recoiled.

"Open it." Mac pounded his legs, bouncing on his knees. "Open it!"

Beau slid his finger under the tape, pulling back the gift wrap.

Page after page detailed the Bell UH-1 Iroquois helicopter, also known as the Huey. Mechanical descriptions, yes, but also the military's history of commissioning them from the Bell aircraft manufacturing company, and then to the way their pilots were chosen.

A small yellow tab protruded from a page farther back, and Beau turned there. Another tab shaped like an arrow pointed to a paragraph. What her read nearly undid him.

Captain Maxwell Cabot was one of the first Huey pilots to be decorated during the conflicts in Nicaragua for extreme bravery in a firefight. Although severely wounded in the leg and hemorrhaging, Captain Cabot kept his craft aloft under enemy fire. Despite dense jungle covering below, he managed to set down and pick up other wounded soldiers in a highly volatile area, evacuating them to the nearest military hospital, saving every one of the wounded soldiers' lives. His helmet was struck by a stray bullet, and pierced the outer edge of his skull, causing unknown internal bleeding, but he continued his flight. For such valor, he was honored by the military and was presented a medal by the U.S. Congress.

Beau reread it.

Dad. Dad was a hero? A respected military officer? All Beau's life, though, Dad had been such a difficult personality. He'd been unpredictable, difficult, and sometimes mean. He'd spent a lot of time drinking, and very little time as a father. Try as he might, Beau had attempted to understand Dad, even going so far as joining up in the Reserve Officers Training Corps. But nothing he experienced in the military excused the way Dad had been at home with Beau or with Mom while they stayed married.

Until now.

Beau swallowed hard, now not even trying to keep the gush of saltwater from leaving his eyes as he read on and on, paragraph after paragraph detailing Dad's heroism. The author had even interviewed him, asking if Dad had any regrets.

Just one, he'd responded. That he'd given too much of himself to the battle and was left with too little afterward.

Beau sat back, staring at the pages, his skin vibrating.

Dad might not have been Beau's hero, exactly, but he'd been a hero and a savior to the men he'd rescued that day. Injured, both in body and mind, he'd pressed on, maybe even doing the best he could under the circumstances, for the remainder of his life.

Dad had given his all, back in that jungle.

The technology Tazewell was making now would have helped Dad see beneath the canopy to where the guns aimed at him lay. *Oh, Dad.*

For a long moment, Beau rested his head in his hands, letting understanding wash through him. Letting forgiveness wash him clean.

Sophie. She hadn't given him a book. She'd given him, for the first time in Beau's life, a reason to understand, love, and respect Dad.

A lump formed in his throat.

"Daddy? Are you okay? You look like you're … crying."

Beau wiped the moisture from his cheeks. "I'm fine. This is a cool book, right?" He held it up for the kids for a second, but they were more interested in the books about dinosaurs or unicorns and other mythical creatures. "She knew me."

"Aunt Sophie loves you, Daddy." Adele hugged him, squishing the book off his lap.

She did. She had to. Right?

All that stuff about the other guy and missing him—it couldn't be as real as what Beau had with Sophie.

"I need to get her back." Real Beau looked up from the page. "She has to come back."

The kids stopped reading. Adele shut her book. "Aunt Sophie?"

"Yeah." He scrubbed his hand over his head. "I need her." He needed her in every aspect of his life. Plus, he wanted her—all of her beautiful, incredible soul.

"Um, Daddy." Mac frowned. "I want her back, too, but Adele wrecked it."

"Hey!" Adele punched his arm. "You wrecked it, too. You're the one who told her you'd rather have a scary spider lady with a cute dog than Aunt Sophie."

"Hey." Mac frowned and folded his arms.

Beau had no idea how to accomplish it, but he'd figure it out. He was Real Beau now—especially minus the weight of the grudge against Dad.

The kids got a little restless and started digging around in the discarded wrapping paper under the tree to see if any presents remained. Beau had, after all, been reading about Dad for a few minutes.

"Are there any presents from Mom?"

There were not. *Come on, Tracey. Not even an acknowledgment of them for Christmas Day?*

His phone chimed.

"Maybe that's Mommy!" Adele said. "Or Sophie!"

It wasn't from either of them. It was from Olympia instead. *Does the fact I don't want to read it tell me anything? Like there's not really room in my heart for her?*

"It's not from Sophie." Adele frowned, looking over Beau's shoulder, and turned on her little adult voice again. "It's from the spider lady with the dog. It's about the surprise she promised. Or should I say, *threatened?*"

"Adele." Enough of that. Beau opened the text.

Are you ready? Say you are because it's time for the shock and pleasure of your holiday.

The doorbell rang. Beau sprang to his feet. "Kids. You. Stay. Here." The words shock and pleasure did not bode well. Olympia had high shock potential. And her idea of pleasure might not be fit for children's viewing hour. "I'll get the door. You guys, er, gather up the trash, okay?" He was jogging now. He threw the door wide, bracing himself for anything.

152

Well, almost anything.

"Hi, honey. I'm home."

"Tracey?"

"Mommy?" one kid hollered. "Mommy!" the other yelled.

"Can I come in?"

Chapter 23

Beau

"Fa-la-la-la-la, la-la, la-la." The kids and Tracey laughed and kept doubling the la-la-las over and over. Tracey, for the first time since Mac was an infant, actually looked happy in her motherhood.

It was strange. Foreign.

Beau didn't trust it.

"I brought you guys some presents." Tracey grinned. From her purse, she pulled out two bags of airline pretzels, presenting them to the kids with all ceremony and dignity. "From the friendly skies. These snacks *have been across the ocean.*"

Beau jerked. "You were overseas?"

"Um, London. The tour's last stop before that you-know-what fired his whole band and his manager and proclaimed he was going solo. Solo, meaning he was dumping me and picking up three teenage British girls."

"Gross!" Adele yelled.

Where had she learned that word?

"That's what I said." Tracey reached out and tickled Adele. "You remembered."

Uh, when had Tracey said that? "Did you and Adele talk recently?"

Adele nodded like her head was on a wind-up toy's motor. "I told Mommy all about our fun Christmas here at Turtledove Place. Like the cookies and the charades and the frozen waterfall Pegasus lights and the swimming with Aunt Sophie in her cool blue swimsuit and the tree you cut down. I told her all of it."

All of it, huh. Right down to the *cool blue swimsuit.* Leave it to Adele.

"Nice pretzels." Beau was less impressed with things that were unimpressive than his kids were.

154

Leaving Tracey and Beau to talk alone, the kids took their special international delicacies to dance to Nero music on their mom's phone near the Christmas tree. Southern rock didn't really suit the Christmas spirit. Not in Beau's book.

"Tracey, or is it Racey now? And what happened to the tattoo?" Beau walked into the front room with her, away from the tree and the uneaten meal, cooling on the table. "What's really going on here?"

"Being Racey was a mistake, as was the tattoo, but not quite as big as if it had been a real tattoo and not henna." She snorted with an eye roll. "Anyway, I'm here because I left Nero and his triplets."

"How long ago?"

"A couple of weeks."

Good for her. "But you didn't come back right away."

"I ..." She closed her eyes and exhaled.

"You were waiting to see if he'd beg for you to come back to him." Like Beau had waited for Tracey. Having been on the other end of that equation, he knew. It was crushing. No wonder she looked so haggard. "While I don't really like you very much, as you know, I do get what you're going through. I'm glad you came back to see the kids. They missed you."

"Oh, pshaw. They had fun, younger women entertaining them." She rolled her eyes. "So did you, I assume. All those hot young things parading around this big place, acting like stand-in wives."

Beau blinked hard. "Are you accusing me of ..."

"Entertaining the nannies? Beau. Please. That's what everyone gets nannies for."

She was so messed up. How could he have married this woman? "Tracey, we'd better change the subject before I lose my temper." It was Christmas, after all. And he'd spent the last month working like crazy to give the kids their best holiday ever. He'd ruin all that if he called their biological mother the names hovering on the tip of his tongue.

"If you weren't dallying with them, why did Adele mention Sophie's swimsuit. Two pieces? Made of strings?" Tracey rolled her eyes again. She had that down to an art. Much like a fifteen-year-old girl. "I bet that was a gift-bow you didn't take long to untie. Sophie always had a crush on you. She could barely hide her jealousy the day I married you."

She had? Always? That wasn't the point right now. He filed it away.

"Don't pretend to be surprised, Beau. She was hot for you from the second she laid eyes on you. Why do you think I kept you two apart the second she grew a chest?"

Tracey had been the one who'd pushed Sophie away from their home? Meanwhile, Sophie had felt banished and rejected. It was so wrong—and based on envy of Sophie's appearance? Geez. "I was married to you, Tracey. I wasn't looking at your sister."

"You would have been."

He stifled a growl. Her retroactive jealousy was killing him. Maybe he should have been looking at Sophie instead, waited for her to grow up instead of assuming Tracey and the brilliant little plane-enthusiast in that school class were anything alike.

But facts remained and needed to be plainly stated. "I didn't unwrap any presents or untie any bows." Beau's teeth clenched. "Why did you come back here?" The pretzels for Christmas gag proved it had nothing to do with her love for their children. She'd better not attempt that lie with him. "There has to be a reason. Are you homeless?"

"As a matter of fact …" She looked at her shoes. Those looked expensive, if impractical for the snow of Sugarplum Falls.

"What."

"I mean, all these years, Beau, you and I scraped by in that little house together. I hated it. I sold it the second I won it in the divorce settlement, so you have to know how much I loathed it, despite the few good memories we made there."

"Few?" Well, they were growing more and more minuscule in Beau's memory the longer Tracey talked. "We spent holidays in that house. The kids learned to ride bikes there, climb trees and play pirates with us." And yet Tracey was more or less calling it a hovel, rather than the home it had been?

"Speaking of learning things, I noticed Mac is talking right. Finally. See? I just had to go away and he's cured." She laughed—an ignorant, careless laugh. "But the point is, the second I leave, you level up and become a mansion-owning landowner of the nicest house around. Pool and everything. Though, you'd better not dive in with any more nannies down there when I come back. At least not so I know about it. I'm very jealous—if you slip up and let me find out."

"I've never cheated on you." Beau's jaw felt tight. That knot in his shoulder was coming back, too. *And Sophie is gone. The knot might be wedged in my muscle forever.* "I was a hundred percent true to what I thought you and I had." Mistakenly thought, that was.

"That's your sad luck with women, is all I can say." She smirked. Oh, to be able to wipe that smirk off her face and down onto her stupid shoe. "So, you're a saint. Is that what you want me to admit? That I was always the wrong one? That you were always right? Is that what it will take to let me move in here with you?"

"Move in?"

"You know. Play house, without the fringe benefits, if you're not into them anymore. I'd be like a roommate. Do a little socializing, host parties, finally get that lifestyle YouTube channel I've been dying to start up. I mean, I should parlay my fifteen minutes of fame as Nero's Noodge, as they called me, into something, don't you think?"

How could Beau answer?

"One thing's for sure. I'll definitely redecorate—get rid of all this old-fashioned décor for you. I never liked all the ridiculous birds, anyway. Someone had an obsession." She snickered, and it was low, callous, mean.

"Tracey? You're not moving in here."

"Beau, you won't deny me what I want." She walked two fingers up his arm. It was more like the itsy bitsy spider than a seduction to him, though, and he cringe-shuddered. "I'm your goddess, remember?"

If that had ever been the case, he'd absolutely forgotten. "No one is redecorating. You're of course allowed to see the children. We can arrange that with the courts."

"Courts!" She snorted. "When I'm living here, I'll see them anytime I want to—or not. The nanny can handle them. Or there's always boarding school. Hey, isn't this the year when you find out if Tazewell is going to come into that cool eight hundred million-dollar contract? It is. Totally! If that's our financial situation, boarding school expenses won't be a drop in the ocean."

"Adele and Mac aren't going to boarding school. Adele just won her school's spelling bee."

"I know, since she wouldn't stop yammering about it."

With every word that came from her mouth, he came closer to requesting a restraining order against her.

"I don't know why you're being so difficult, Beau. I was told—on good authority—that you miss me. That you wanted me back, that you want our family to be intact again."

The words stopped Beau like a truck. "Excuse me?" Who would have told Tracey that? "Have you been talking to Sophie?" Why would Sophie foist Tracey on him? Was it just so she could get away from him, and resume her life without the struggle of constant childcare?

"Of course I've been talking to Sophie. I can't get *away* from talking to Sophie. She's forever calling me and then putting Adele on the phone. Like I said, *yammering.*" Tracey sounded exhausted by her own daughter's excitement. "But it's not Sophie who told me. I wouldn't have believed *her.*"

"Who, then? Your mom? The kids?"

"I wouldn't have believed them either. I'm talking about *good authority,* Beau." Tracey paused for dramatic effect. "Olympia Barron told me, okay?"

"Olympia!" But ... but ... Olympia had been flirting with Beau mercilessly. She'd been more or less climbing his ankle with her toes the other night, offering to loosen him up. *What do you really want, Beau?* she'd asked. "Oh." *Ohhhh.* Beau had answered that he wanted an intact family.

And Olympia had said she'd do anything to make that happen.

That must have meant up to and including calling Tracey and convincing her Beau wanted Tracey back. It may have included telling Sophie she wasn't wanted.

Oh, Beau had really messed this up. Not on purpose, but the result was the same.

"I'll be having words with Olympia," he ground out. "Turtledove Place

158

can't be your home, Tracey."

"But—but Beau! What about what Olympia said? I told her I could do monogamy, probably, for your sake—especially for a shot at this luxurious lifestyle. Seriously, Beau. What have you got to lose? Let's give it a shot."

"You may have made a long trip to get here, across the ocean, pretzels and all, but you know I can't live like that. It's not right." Not when someone else had his heart. "In fact, it's wrong." And a terrible example for the kids.

"Beau! I put up with your poverty. I stayed with you when you were a lowly first lieutenant. We lived on nothing for ages. Now you're living in a seven-bedroom mansion and you expect me to just walk out on that? You owe me, Beau. I paid for this with my blood, sweat, and tears."

"It's not happening. Not like that. Now, if you want to stay for Christmas dinner, read stories to the kids, maybe build a snowman like they have been begging to do, we could try to give them Christmas."

"I'm a give and take person, Beau. I'll give you that, but you'd better believe I'll take what's coming to me, too." She looked around at the house. "Those stupid pigeons will have to go, though. Non-negotiable."

"Us getting back together—that's the thing that's non-negotiable. And you'll never live in this house."

"Beau."

"I'm not budging."

"But you always budge."

"Not anymore. You're the one who needs to change, Tracey. For the kids."

She snorted. "They don't even know I'm alive. They couldn't miss me, even if I tried to make them. But you will. You'll see. You'll be calling me, begging me to come back. But I won't come. You're not a rock star. Don't go thinking I'll be at your beck and call."

She was leaving again? Just like that? He exhaled. Hurricane Tracey had done her damage and was blowing out of town again.

"Mommy!" Adele came running back in from the Nero dance party near the tree. "Read me this story from Aunt Sophie? It's about a little girl who loves to spell and wins the spelling bee."

Tracey's sneer grew. "If Aunt Sophie gave you a book, she'd better be the one stuck on the couch reading it to you." She looked at her phone. "It turns out, I need to be back in London right away. You guys *love* those pretzels, okay?"

"You're leaving, Mommy?" Adele looked wounded.

"I just came to say Merry Christmas." She put her coat back on. "Tell Mac to keep working on his letter R sounds, okay? He can surprise me when I come again." She was at the door, and Adele was chasing after her.

"But when, Mommy? When are you coming back?"

"Not sure. Bye, sugar. Be good for your dad." And she was on the porch, with Beau alone. "Don't think you can just replace me with Sophie. I have it from my dad that her doctor boyfriend is meeting Mom and Dad today, and she's meeting his parents, and it's serious between them, so extinguish that gleam in your lecherous eye that you always had for my little sister, Beau. Forget her. She's gone."

That was so true it stung.

Chapter 24

Beau

The kids were in bed, finally, Mac hugging his Huey helicopter that he refused to put down. "I am glad Mommy came for dinner. Except, she forgot to eat with us. I bet she's hungry."

Yep, and her gullet would never be full. *You can never get enough of what you don't need, because what you don't need can never satisfy you.*

Beau dragged himself down the stairs of the cavernous mansion, a tiredness in him he hadn't felt in months. Tracey always hollowed him out, leaving him like the craggy hull of an emptied walnut shell. The Christmas tree lights blinked as if to remind him *Sophie's gone, Sophie's gone, Sophie's gone.* Could Tracey's assertion be real—that Sophie had met that other man's parents today, and that the guy had asked Mr. Hawkins for permission to propose to her?

Well, it made sense that any red-blooded male with a brain in his head would be crazy not to want Sophie. She was the real deal, inside and out.

Beyond the Christmas tree, the house was dim, and far too quiet after the commotion of the day. Nothing looked good in the fridge, even though Beau had only picked at his turkey dinner when Tracey blew out of the house.

Eventually, he found himself on the sofa in the living room staring at the sooty black grate of the fireplace, alone on the couch where he'd last held Sophie.

Three dates—pseudo-dates but dates nonetheless—and a kiss. She'd awakened a sleeping self he'd more or less forgotten. She'd given him back his fatherhood mojo, his love for Christmas, his swagger, his identity as Captain Beau Cabot. *She believed in me, so I could too.*

But she'd slipped through his fingers—almost imperceptibly. Which was stupid because she'd been right *here*, at Turtledove Place, day after day to the point he'd taken for granted that she'd be waiting for him with breakfast in the morning, taking care of the kids after school, watching over their family's needs on almost every front. Until—*poof!* She wasn't.

It might be easy to shift the blame to the kids for their rash words about wanting a mommy, but on their own, those were transparent enough Sophie would have seen through them. No, the real blame lay with Beau for not seizing the moment, for not recognizing and owning up to his growing feelings in time to catch her. For not pouncing on the moment that she wavered about their physical relationship's escalation and convincing her it was not, in fact, a mistake on her part or his or theirs as a couple. It was an obvious progression based on their shared lives, interests, and love.

Love? Yeah. That was the correct term for it. He did love his kids, and he'd somewhat loved Tracey—though she was more or less a murderer of love. However, until he'd felt the abiding, soul-feeding love of Sophie Hawkins, Beau had never been on the receiving end of real romantic love. With her, it wasn't merely the flutters and blood-rush of seeing a knee-weakening hourglass figure in a swimsuit, or the daily grind of working together toward a common goal like raising children, although it was both of those things. It was the magic that came when those worlds collided, and when an additional element of shared minds was added. Sophie had always been interested in the things that fascinated Beau, like aviation. She'd appreciated the things he valued, like the love that built Turtledove Place. If he continued to get to know her, chances were strong there were hundreds if not thousands of additional connection points between him and this beautiful woman.

Who had slipped away from him, leaving him even more lonely than when his marriage had fallen apart and his mother died.

Knowing love and then losing it wasn't better than never having experienced love at all, in spite of what the old adage asserted. It was far worse.

Beau hadn't cried at his mother's funeral. Tracey's exit had left him too raw, too wrung out for getting weepy. But his tear ducts activated now. He swatted at his eyes, nose and cheeks to make the emotion stop.

I do love her. The admission sliced, like a paper cut. *I need her. I want her. And she's gone.*

There had to be a way to rewind the calendar and go back to their kiss. Or to stop the wheels of whatever bus she was on now from turning. He couldn't think. His brain was too full of the spreading bruise of regrets.

The empty hearth gaped at him like a dark maw, threatening to swallow him whole—until. Yeah. The hearth was exactly what he needed.

Beau leaped up, set a fire with two hickory logs, and some kindling. In no time, that grate held a roaring blaze, and shortly, it became a mellow glow. Real Beau had resurrected in front of this fire, while wrapped in Sophie's soft arms and drinking in her perfect kisses.

Soon, the glow and the memory, as well as the longing and the need, opened the locked boxes of Beau's brain. He was going to take matters into his own hands and bring Sophie's and his relationship back to this hearth as well.

He knew exactly how he was going to make it happen. To make her his.

Starting tonight.

Chapter 25

Sophie

Usually by nightfall on Christmas, Sophie was exhausted and ready to fall into bed in a post-joy coma. Not tonight. Tonight, she lay on her bed and stared out the french doors to the orange streetlight's glow coming through from the balcony and counted her losses, rather than her gains. All she wanted was to crawl inside a movie-binge and hook herself up to a chocolate IV. But even that would take too much effort.

Without Beau and the kids, nothing felt right. In fact, everything felt wrong. If she were a different person, Sophie would stomp right out of this room, drive to Sugarplum Falls and give Beau a piece of her mind. She'd tell him Olympia Barron was a hundred percent the wrong person to raise Mac and Adele, and while the woman may be as alluring as a siren, she could never nurture them in the ways they needed. In fact, she'd likely send them off to private schools so she wouldn't have to bother with them.

Then who would raise them, comfort them, feed and help and love them?

Ooh! There was an idea. Maybe Beau would let Sophie raise them. Loan them out to her for the next ten years. She could do it. She'd just have to … no. They needed their dad in their lives. Sophie could sub in as a mom, but not as a father, too.

Her eyes hurt when she closed them. Probably from the crying jag she'd been on all afternoon, ever since—

Plink! Something hit the window of her french doors. *Plink, plink!* Something else hit it. Hail? No! Mother Nature's worst precipitation. The ice chunks of destruction. Wouldn't a hailstorm just be the most fitting ending to this most terrible day?

Plink!

Sophie wrenched herself out of bed, grabbed slippers and a robe, and went to check it out. She might have to bring in her potted plants to keep them

164

from getting ruined. The french door creaked when she opened it, and—

A guitar strummed below, a soft chord. "Chestnuts roasting on an open fire." A man stood in the shadows of the evergreen oak but stepped into the orange glow of the streetlight for the second chord and line of lyrics about Jack Frost nipping at noses.

Beau? Sophie's heart tipped over in her chest, and she clutched it so it wouldn't go tumbling out. "Beau?"

"Yuletide carols being sung ..." A sheepish grin tugged at a side of his face. "By me, actually."

He was singing. With his guitar. Below Sophie's balcony. She tugged her pajamas tighter around her waist, hugging herself. Was this real or a dream?

"So I'm offering this simple phrase," he sang on, through the entire song, in his clear, resonant voice. Softly, though—thank goodness, since it was coming up on midnight. "Merry Christmas to you." It sounded like love.

Sophie blinked, trying to decipher whether it was a dream or a dream come true.

"Beau, what are you doing here?" she stage-whispered. A dog barked in the distance. It was cold. Not Sugarplum Falls cold, but definitely a cold night. "Come inside."

"Not yet." He strummed again, this time breaking into "Let it Snow." After that, he gave her a chorus of "An Old-Fashioned Christmas."

"Beau, is it just me, or do all of the songs you chose mention fireplaces?"

"I'm pretty transparent, aren't I?"

Sneaky. And gorgeous. And singing to her. Every shiver in the world ran across her skin.

"I'm going to end with this," Beau said, strumming a new set of chords.

"Good!" a neighbor shouted. "Then will you please take your music elsewhere?"

Wow, Darlington was not like Sugarplum Falls. "Sorry!" she shouted. "Um, Merry Christmas?"

"It will be when it's quiet."

Beau strummed a chord. "I'll be home for Christmas," he sang, and Sophie's heart rent in two. It was a military soldier's song to his family back home. "You can count on me."

He hung on the word *lovelight*. If Sophie stood just right, lovelight did gleam from him. Could it be real? She pinched herself hard.

I'm so glad I had the courage to turn down Matt. That had all happened today. A million years ago today, but she'd let him go. Rightly, but not easily. He was such a good man. *He will find the right woman for him. She's out there. Just like I told him today, but that my heart was taken, whether I liked it or not, by someone I couldn't have.*

Except, maybe she could! Beau sang on, finishing the song, and Sophie swayed to the rhythms of Beau's tenor voice.

"Sophie?" he asked in the cold air, his breath hanging as steam. "It won't be *home* at Christmas. Not without you. It wasn't today, and it never can be."

What was he saying? That he wanted her back? "Beau, I—"

"Stop. I don't want to hear any excuses about any bosses or people named Matt. All of that needs to be put on a back burner while you give me a chance to prove myself to you—and while you find out that I'm really the right man for you. That Adele and Mac are as important in your life as you are in theirs. They love you, have been asking for you, and they need you."

"Where are they? Is anyone watching them?"

"They're safe with my aunt, Elaine."

"Beau ..." She couldn't speak, since her throat was filling with love and hope.

This is my moment. It was everything she'd ever waited for. She should go to him.

"Just a minute, please." *I love him. I always have.* Grabbing a jacket, she slipped on some shoes, and raced downstairs.

Beau and his guitar leaned against his SUV. He'd put on a sheepskin-lined denim jacket and looked like a dream come true. She tiptoed up to him, holding her breath.

"Your songs ... Thank you." They meant everything to her. "I—you say the kids missed me?"

"They need you. It's not just the kids who need you, Sophie. It's not just the kids who love you." He reached for both her hands. Sophie had to squeeze them tight to steady herself.

Was he saying what it sounded like he was saying? Every cell in her body vibrated to know what he might say next. *Say it, please, please, please.*

Beau met her gaze, an intensity there that she'd never felt from him before. "I love you, Sophie."

He said it. He meant it. *He loves me.* She soared like the F-16 Fighting Falcon. She floated like the E-3 Sentry AWACS. *I can't believe it.*

But Beau went on. "You're the best gift of Christmas—and of my life. You gave me exactly what I needed."

"You liked the book?" Oh, she'd been so worried it was too personal.

"Yes, but I'm not talking about the book. I'm talking about the gift of yourself—and of myself when I'm with you. I feel like myself again. That's the gift of real love—which was the first gift of Christmas."

And then, he was kissing her, in the cold night air. This was so different from the brain-stealing fireplace-drunk make-out, although that had been amazing. As his lips lightly brushed hers, and then pressed serenely, this kiss was different. It was eddies of snow flurries as he teased, then coaxed, and then enveloped her. It was storm clouds and clear days at the same time. When he placed one hand behind her head, and another at her waist, it was wind and light and rain. When he pulled her tight and deepened the kiss, it was all the blinking lights on every Christmas tree. Beau's kiss of real love took her to new heights of belief in herself, in him, in forever.

In a breath between kisses, she whispered, "I love you, too, Beau. I have for a long time."

He trailed a few kisses along her cheek and her eyebrows. "Oh?" He kissed her softly on the lips again. "How long?"

"Longer than long." She kissed his temple, and he pressed a supple kiss to her throat. "But not as long as I plan to love you."

"Oh?" he asked. "How long is that?"

"As long as Sugar Lake spills over Sugarplum Falls. As long as gravity tugs downward and air and speed follow the principles lift."

"You're the lift, Sophie. Thank you." He kissed her again.

Chapter 26

Beau

New Year's Eve came quickly, now that time could fly when he was having fun again. Sophie made everything fun—not just for the kids, either. He shot a glance at the beautiful woman in the seat beside him. Yeah, very fun. She'd brought sparkle back to his life. She'd brought *him* back to his life.

However, this moment wasn't exactly the excitement the past few days had been, as Beau gripped the wheel of his SUV as he headed up the canyon above the town of Sugarplum Falls. Though he'd been basking in Sophie's attention all week, not even Sophie's peaceful presence could overcome his tension right now—because at five o'clock, just minutes from now, the DoD contract winner would be announced.

Why the government could announce an award on New Year's Eve and not on Christmas Eve or any of the days in between, Beau had no idea. However, they'd received a direct e-mail from the dot-gov agency that alerted applicants to announcements, and this was their day.

But for Beau, there was a lot more on his mind for New Year's Eve than even the contract award. *I'm not letting a Sugarplum Falls tradition go to waste.* And his chemistry with Sophie definitely wouldn't allow for another year to pass for the moment to arrive again. Not if he wanted to set a good example of marriage for his kids.

Every employee of Tazewell Solutions would be gathered at the annual New Year's Eve dinner at Frosty Ridge Lodge. When the email came telling him about the bad timing that coincided with their holiday party, the employees agreed they'd like to all be present to either celebrate or mourn together.

I pray it's a celebration and not a wake. At least he'd made payroll, thanks to North Star Capital. Beau would feel horrible for asking them to take this risk on him if it didn't pan out. Wyatt North had been incredibly generous to Beau in his direst moment of need when Beau had sought him out at that family wedding, hat in hand.

Worse, the legacy Pops built in his lifetime—besides his happy marriage to Mom—was on the line, and on Beau's shoulders.

For once in his life, however, he didn't feel like he was carrying the burden alone.

He parked the car and helped Sophie out of the passenger side.

"Isn't four o'clock early for an employee dinner?" Sophie asked, walking beside him into Frosty Ridge.

"It's a holiday. Pops never wanted to intrude on people's other traditions, if they had them. However, he also liked to take time to celebrate the wins by looking back on the year. Celebrations, to him, meant good food." And Jordan McNair's cooks at Frosty Ridge made the best steaks in town—among other dishes. Despite the earliness of dinner, Beau planned on staying through the New Year's Eve ball Frosty Ridge Lodge was hosting, right until midnight. No way was he squandering a minute of his first night out alone with the woman he loved. "Thank you for coming with me."

"I wouldn't miss it."

"I don't mean just tonight. I mean back to Sugarplum Falls." He and Sophie had spent the entirety of the kids' Christmas break together, watching movies with them, baking, even doing a little singing. It turned out, he didn't mind singing anymore. "It's been an amazing week."

Sophie paused as they reached the top step before opening the doors to the lodge. She rose up on tiptoe and kissed him softly. "Like I say, I wouldn't miss it."

"Well, well." Up walked Olympia. "Exactly as I suspected."

"Olympia." Ire bubbled to Beau's surface. He hadn't chewed her out on Christmas Day for her stunt in telling Tracey that Beau wanted her back, as it was *Christmas*. But he also hadn't run into her since to give him the piece of his mind she deserved. "I think we have a few personal things to discuss."

Olympia held up a red-silk gloved hand. "Please. I'm the one who needs to speak—to Sophie." She turned to Sophie, and before Beau could leap in and prevent the attack, Olympia said. "I owe you a huge apology."

Sophie cocked her head to the side, but didn't speak.

Olympia continued. "I was operating under a set of mistaken perceptions about Beau, about your sister, and about you. Beau told me, as I said, that he wouldn't consider starting a real family with one of his nannies, so I moved a few chess pieces around without realizing that you, Sophie, were not a nanny. You were his children's aunt. More than that, you were his soul's balm. Please forgive me."

When Sophie gave a slight nod, Olympia leaned in and gave her one of her signature each-cheek European air-kiss. "Thank you. I couldn't stand the thought of going into a new year with bad feelings looming between you and me. Beau means too much to me. We're business partners, and I admire him to the moon and back. His happiness is key to Tazewell's success—and I mean that literally." She looked around. "Now, where is that irresistible Jordan McNair? If he's not taken, I plan to catch his eye tonight."

Jordan wasn't taken. But was he a good fit for Olympia? Maybe no one in this town was sophisticated enough for her. But no question, if she wanted to catch a man's eye, the woman had the skill set.

"Color me dumbfounded," Sophie said as she handed her coat over the counter at the coat check. "I did not expect that even a little bit."

"Me, neither."

"I underestimated her, I'll admit."

Beau underestimated people all the time. Especially Sophie. "You look stunning in that dress."

"Thank you for the gift. I wasn't expecting anything from you. You didn't have to give me something just because I gave you the book."

Oh, yes, he did. "It's a great color on you. I wanted to see you in it again."

She blushed. "I did notice it's the same color as my, er, swimsuit."

Ah, apparently that wasn't lost on her. "So sue me. I like my woman in blue." The same color of blue he'd been stunned into a lust-coma over in the past. The dress dipped in the front and the back, with straps gathered atop her shoulders by silver rings, also echoes of that other outfit. So sue him. "Sweetwater Boutique custom-tailored it. I wanted you to have something no one else would be wearing tonight."

"I'm glad you like it on me."

Like it. He was ready to stare at it and then get rid of it. "Just when I think you couldn't be more beautiful, you prove me wrong." He'd better focus on the tasks at hand. Because tonight—especially the next thirty minutes of his life—was important for a lot of reasons.

Not just because of the contract announcement. Although, if things went well with that, he'd be free to explore other avenues of his life.

"Thanks for bringing me tonight," Sophie nestled beside him, filling his senses with her perfume and her warmth. "Do you know this is our first date without the children?"

"Thank your friend Vronky for me for taking the kids for the evening."

"She didn't mind. She's been dying to see Turtledove Place and Sugarplum Falls."

The kids knew Vronky, too, from their stays with Sophie in years gone by, so leaving them with her was easy for Beau.

A loud shout broke out in the ballroom. "I guess we'd better see what all the commotion is." Beau pulled Sophie along, speeding toward the noise.

"It's here! It's in!" Aunt Elaine jogged up to Beau the second he set foot in the ballroom. "Have you even been looking at the clock?"

Obsessively, up until a few minutes ago. "Is it five already?"

"It is. Now, just because you've got the prettiest girl ever to set foot in Sugarplum Falls on your arm—and the best one for you, better even than I would have chosen for you myself—doesn't mean you should be killing the rest of us by inches." She slapped him hard on the shoulder.

"I am a weapons and strategic command expert, you know. Killing by inches is something we could specialize in, should we choose." Beau kept Sophie at his side as he approached the open laptop setup waiting for him at the front dais. He took the microphone.

"Open the email already! I almost clicked on it myself, but I still have some scruples, and you're the boss." Elaine pinched his elbow, and then she went to stand beside Olympia. Everyone in the ballroom seemed to be in lines and gripping hands.

At least the staff understood the importance of this moment.

"Everyone, thank you for coming." Beau's microphone squeaked once, and everyone hushed. "Without any speeches, since every single one of you here has worked tirelessly for six years on this project and knows what's at stake, I'll simply open the email." He indicated the white wall space behind him where a laptop's screen was being projected. He logged in and then opened his e-mail inbox. "Here goes everything."

Sophie squeezed his free hand, as though she could inject all her energy and prayers into creating the ached-for results in Tazewell's favor.

With his other hand, he clicked the message. Words blurred, but then they focused, and Beau read them aloud to the assemblage. "This is to inform you that Tazewell Solutions' software has been selected to be developed and placed on all military aircraft for the strategic defense and tactical ..."

Beau could have read more, including the insanely large amount of financial compensation, but everyone was cheering too loudly and he wouldn't have been heard. But also, because his mouth was otherwise occupied with Sophie's elated, exquisite kiss.

He encircled her in his arms, kissed her until he couldn't breathe, and then said into the long, pale-blonde strands of hair beside her ear. "It's thanks to you."

"Me? I didn't do anything."

"You did everything. You changed me." He gazed at her, and a heat filled his chest and torso like he'd never felt. But it wasn't just temperature, it was pure, bone-melting love. In that second, Real Beau fully re-inhabited his body, and took control of his speech capabilities. "Sophie, it's sudden, but it's also New Year's Eve in Sugarplum Falls. Most guys wait until midnight during the ball here at Frosty Ridge Lodge, but I need to ask you now."

He glided to one knee, almost bowing in reverence at the pooling folds of her beautiful blue gown and in the glow of her excited but hesitant gaze. From his suit coat pocket extracted a blue velvet box. He cracked it wide and sent a prayer heavenward. *Let her say yes.* "Sophie Hawkins, will you belong to me?"

"I always have." She kissed him like she meant it.

Epilogue

Beau

Christmastime, The Following Year

"You're saying I have to throw enough snowballs at this Mr. Snowman monstrosity to bust open the lowest section of his belly? That sounds like destruction of property. Or … murder."

Adele giggled. "It's only snow, Daddy."

He loved that she was ten already and still called him Daddy. How long would that last? She'd be a teenager before he could blink. Mac, too.

But luckily, whatever little bonus family member is growing inside Sophie, due to my highly willing help, gives us a fresh start. And once he or she was born, maybe they could give baby-making a few more tries.

Beau stacked up several more snowballs for his arsenal. Sophie sat nearby on the bench at the edge of the woods overlooking Turtledove Place and the view of Sugar Lake, dangling her feet and looking smug.

"Wipe that sneaky look off your face." Beau feigned brandishing a snowball in her direction. "I can't believe you told Mac and Adele the sex of our baby, but I have to undergo a gender reveal game." Didn't this seem wrong to anyone else?

"Just throw the snowball, Dad." So Mac wasn't using Daddy anymore. Fine.

Beau came over first and planted a kiss on Sophie's upturned lips. "Fine. I'm on it."

"I believe in you." Sophie snickered, shooing him back on task. "Start throwing that snow." She gave him a little punch in the arm, possibly as a wee bit of payback for the morning sickness she'd endured for three months running. "Come on, Beau. Fire away."

Standing at the designated distance from Mr. Snowman, Beau threw the first snowball, smacking the formation right in the gut. "Nothing happened." Probably because the powdery snow fluffed apart on impact.

"You have to throw more, Daddy." Adele groaned. "Here, I'll keep making snowballs for you." She sprayed the snow with some water first, to give it enough moisture to become a ball, and dropped it atop the pyramid of ammo he'd already compiled. "Go, go, go!"

Beau threw, and threw, and threw. "I think I see ..." No, he couldn't tell yet. "Come on, guys. Is it pink or blue in there? Can I step closer?"

"No!" Mac and Adele hollered together—one of the few things they did well together. Hollering. They'd have to work on that as a family. Maybe this new baby would be soft-spoken. Fat chance. He or she would have to speak up to ever be heard at all. "Just keep throwing!"

Okay, so he tossed snowball after snowball, until finally—"It's purple." The snow inside the belly of the snowman had been dyed or sprayed or whatever not pink, not blue, but purple.

Mac and Adele snickered, and then they laughed, and then they fell on the ground and rolled with laughter.

"Who came up with this game?" He came over and sprinkled snow all over their faces. "Good trick, kids."

"No, Dad. It's real. We just combined pink and blue because Aunt Sophie is having a pink baby *and* a blue baby."

Pink and blue? What in the ...? "Twins!" Beau whirled around. He ran to Sophie, lifted her in the air, and spun. "It's both? We're having two? At once?" Somehow he developed a high degree of skill in spluttering.

Sophie kissed him, softly at first, and then in a full, luscious, celebratory kiss. "It's the best of everything."

No, Sophie was the best of everything. "Have I told you today that I love you?"

"Do you?"

"And that you're beautiful. That I want to be your man and the father of your twins, and later your triplets."

174

"Triplets! Slow down, Captain."

Triplets would make seven children. Just about right.

When the snow antics ended, the four of them—plus the two inside Sophie—two—*two!*—returned to the house. Good thing Turtledove Place had seven bedrooms. Because it was coming. Yeah, sooner or later.

Tonight was the Hot Cocoa Festival, and then they had a movie on the menu. *And some time next to the fire after the kids went to bed.*

They called Sophie's parents, Mr. & Mrs. Hawkins, with the news. Strange as it should be to be announcing babies with their other daughter, it felt right. Better than right—and Sophie's parents had never balked for a moment about Beau's transference of love.

"They probably don't mind any of our history since Tracey's finally happy," Sophie said after they hung up. "I guess Nero really did love her. And even better, now every day can be Tracey's day, as star of the show."

Good for Tracey—who was happily living on a sparsely inhabited island, hosting a lifestyle program with her new husband. *Rock Star Private Island* was right up her alley. She was a trendsetter in a very small village, and loving every minute of it. Plus, she'd kept her real name and not added any more tattoos, henna or otherwise. She'd even invited Mac and Adele to come make a guest appearance someday.

Beau was still thinking over that offer. Maybe when the twins were born.

"I've been thinking about names," Sophie said, after the kids ran inside to where the fresh-cut Christmas tree waited to be decorated. "What about Dove for the girl? For your grandmother's favorite bird."

Nice. "And Turtle for the boy. It's a perfect match."

"Beau! No!" She pushed him. "Not even Tortuga."

He whipped out his phone and opened one of those multi-lingual translation apps. "If not Tortuga, what about *Skilpadde*. That's Norwegian. Or the Portuguese is great, too. *Tartaruga*."

He named five more, until she stopped his mouth with a kiss.

Yeah, that's what he'd really wanted. Then he rested his forehead against hers, looking her in the eye. "It's amazing creating a family at Turtledove Place together with you."

Thank you for reading *Christmas at Holly Berry Cottage.* To read Beau and Sophie's journey to love and healing at Christmastime in Sugarplum Falls, check out *Christmas at Turtledove Place*, Book 2 in the Sugarplum Falls Romance series. To read Tabitha and Sam's story, check out *Christmas at Angels Landing,* Book 3 in the Sugarplum Falls Romance Series.

Sugarplum Falls Series

Christmas at Holly Berry Cottage
Christmas at Turtledove Place
Christmas at Angels Landing
Christmas at The Cider House (exclusive to newsletter subscribers)
More novels in the series coming soon.

Stay in touch and find out about new clean romance releases. Sign up for Jennifer Griffith's fun, lighthearted newsletter by downloading a free romantic novella from authorjennifergriffith.com.

About the Author

Jennifer Griffith lives in Arizona with her husband, where they are raising their five children to love Christmas. She tries to put more lights on her tree every year, and she wholeheartedly believes the best way to kick off the holiday season is to sing Christmas songs with her husband's extended family for two to three hours on Thanksgiving night. Her favorite carols are "O Holy Night" and "Walking in a Winter Wonderland." She once sang a solo of "Gesu Bambino" that wasn't too bad. The best part of it was her oldest son accompanied her on the piano as she sang the contralto arrangement.

Made in the USA
Middletown, DE
04 March 2021